D1055461

APRIL'S FOOL

Other Books by Blanche Marriott

Kaleidoscope
Way Out West

APRIL'S FOOL

•

Blanche Marriott

AVALON BOOKS

NEW YORK

Published by Avalon Books,
an imprint of Thomas Bouregy & Co., Inc.
New York, NY

Library of Congress Cataloging-in-Publication Data

Marriott, Blanche.
    April's fool / Blanche Marriott.
        p.   cm.
    ISBN 978-0-8034-7614-1 (hardcover : acid-free paper)
    I. Title.
    PS3613.A769A86 2011
    813'.6—dc23

                                        2011025768

PRINTED IN THE UNITED STATES OF AMERICA
ON ACID-FREE PAPER
BY RR DONNELLEY, HARRISONBURG, VIRGINIA

To my niece, Shelley Hart,
the daughter I never had

Prologue

April clutched the embossed white and gold wedding album tightly to her bosom. Once she let go, her friends would see right through her, through the ruse, through the layers of armor she'd protected herself with as each year slipped by and the single life etched another notch on her lonely existence.

She longed for a marriage like her friends had and too often fantasized that she'd be swept off her feet in a whirlwind romance. The phony album was a byproduct of that fantasy. But would they see the April Fool's joke as overindulgent self-pity? Was she that desperate to have a life like everyone else's? The one she'd thought she would have eight years ago?

No matter. She'd come this far; she might as well go all the way.

One more look around at her three best friends who eagerly anticipated her "big vacation news," then she tightened her lips and exhaled with resignation as she lifted the album to the table. Three sets of eyes widened, and the bustling noise of the busy restaurant faded into the background, leaving only the sound of Sharon's gasp as she caught the words on the cover.

Quickly, before anyone had a chance to speak, Michelle grabbed the book and flipped it open, seconding Sharon's gasp.

"You're married?"

Chapter One

So the old man was finally retiring.

Michael Goode shook his head at the executive memo and rubbed his forehead in amazement. Not that he wanted him gone; it was just that Howard Gellar had been threatening this for years while the investment firm continued its fast-paced growth in Providence's business mainline, due in large part to Michael's aggressive foresight.

He'd become both the engine and caboose, leading everyone in the firm with new client acquisitions and pushing those on the bottom to heights they'd never realized they could achieve. Even though Michael wore the crown of top moneymaker at year-end, Howard Gellar still held the record for lifetime average.

But at last Howard had set a date—less than a year from now, at the end of next tax season. April 15 seemed an appropriate demarcation for this fiscal legend whose respected reputation spread as far as Boston, New York, and Washington, D.C.

The retirement date also defined an accelerated timeline for Michael's future and his game plan to be named Gellar's successor. Ever confident, Michael knew he could achieve anything he set his mind to. He always had, ever since his high school debate team chose him for their leader in his sophomore year. From there, his life had been one success story after another.

With a rush of air from Michael's office door, Kenny Gellar, the not-so-aggressive competitor in Michael's planned rise up the corporate ladder, breezed in. *Competitor* because he happened to be Howard's nephew, *not-so-aggressive* because, even though his short resume depicted a savvy investment advisor, he rarely exhibited enough motivation for any upward movement.

Lucky for Michael. That meant Howard funneled all the promising new clients to him and left the tried-and-true ones for Kenny. Michael ate up each new challenge, hungry to satisfy the overachiever within. Time and again Gellar's fatherly clap on the back assured him he was headed in the right direction. He had the world at his fingertips, and nothing could distract him from his rise to the top.

"You're married?" Kenny's abrupt burst to get the question out nearly bowled Michael from his seat. "I can't believe you didn't tell anyone—even me! When did this happen?" He dropped a heavy photo album onto Michael's thick mahogany desk, sending a parade of yellow pencils rolling to the edge of the immaculately polished top.

Confused by the inquisition and by the large white and gold album with its title *Our Wedding* glaring at him, Michael brusquely rescued the pencils and set them back in a straight line with his blotter. An orderly desk for an orderly mind. Then, blinking away his annoyance, he frowned up at his co-worker.

"What are you talking about? You know I'm not married. Who told you that?"

"No one told me. I saw it for myself." Kenny poked an adamant finger at the wedding album.

Certain that Kenny had had a "light" lunch, Michael decided he'd take the bait and have a look at the incriminating evidence. Rolling his leather executive chair forward, he flipped open the thick cover to see himself dressed in a tux and standing head to head with a beautiful, golden-curls-coiffed bride. They each held a glass of Champagne while staring into each other's eyes. He noted her sensual appeal, inviting yet discreet.

He turned the page. There they were, dancing under a huge crystal chandelier. A violinist played in the background. The scene tugged at his memory, but he couldn't make sense of the illogical image.

"Kenny, where did you get this?"

"So you're not denying it?"

"Of course I'm denying it. I'm not married, never have been, have no intentions. Now, where did you get it?"

Kenny nodded. "That was my first reaction. I mean, how could you be married and none of us know it? Then I remembered your secret weekend away last month, all your hush-hush plans. I thought, well, maybe it was a rushed marriage, and you were too embarrassed to tell the old man."

Michael shot up from his seat and grabbed the album. "That's insane!" Just as that weekend had been. Yeah, he'd been secretive, but only because it'd been a fact-finding mission, a job offer from one of his clients. He'd intentionally led Kenny to believe he'd gone on a romantic rendezvous and had dodged the prying questions for a solid week afterward.

"Then explain those pictures."

Sidestepping to the floor-length window with its high-altitude view of busy Providence, Rhode Island, Michael looked at the bride and groom cutting the cake and struggled to remember why it struck a familiar chord.

"I can't. Will you please tell me where you got this?"

"It came by messenger just a few minutes ago."

Michael snapped his head up from the pictures, certain he'd heard wrong. "Messenger? You're joking, right?"

"Not a chance. I was at the reception desk when Shelley signed for it. She opened it, read the note, skimmed the pictures, and gave me the most scalding, silent reprimand, as though I'd told the lie of the century."

"Note? What note?"

Kenny reached into his pocket, then dropped a folded paper onto the desk. "It says the album was found at the Over The Edge restaurant. Since there were no names inside, they held on to it for a few weeks until one of the waitresses inspected it more carefully and recognized you. She knew you worked here but didn't know your name, so they forwarded it with this note of explanation."

Michael shook his head, studying the next photo of him kissing the bride. No sense. It made no sense at all.

"Kenny, if I didn't know you better, I'd think you were playing a sick joke, but this just isn't your style. Yet, it does seem to be someone's idea of a joke."

"But whose? Why would someone want to see you married?"

"I guess I'll have to find that out. Any ideas on where I should start?"

Kenny edged closer, peering over Michael's shoulder. "You *do* make a handsome groom." Michael elbowed him, a warning that *groom* was not in his past or future vocabulary. "You want me to lie? Geez, I mean, come on, who wouldn't look great in a tux, kissing a beautiful woman like that?" He moved closer and spoke in a low tone. "You really don't know anything about this? Do you even know the bride?"

"No!"

"Okay, don't shoot the messenger."

Michael turned the last page. The bride and groom waved to the guests as they left the reception. Again, the scene seemed familiar, but he was at a loss to nail it down. As he flipped the parchment covering the last page, a small notation at the bottom caught his eye. *April's Fool* had been neatly handwritten and underlined. He frowned at the disturbing insinuation.

Beside him, Kenny exhaled a low whistle. "I didn't notice that before. I wonder what it means."

Michael slammed the book shut and tossed it onto the desk. "It means somebody is making a fool of me."

"That's crazy. Who would do a thing like that? I mean, you said you don't know her, right? You had nothing to do with it, right? There has to be a logical explanation. How can you be in a photo with a perfect stranger—"

Kenny stopped midsentence. His forehead wrinkled. His eyes squinted. He flipped open the cover again and stared at the smiling couple.

"What? What is it?" Michael asked suspiciously. "Do you know something?"

"I didn't notice it before, but I think I *do* recognize the bride. April. There's a girl named April downstairs at Web Works, and *this* looks like her."

"Web Works? I don't know anyone named April. I don't even know anyone at Web Works." Although it was the company that handled the firm's Web site, Michael didn't have much contact with them. Sales and marketing kept their fingers in that exclusive pie.

"No, me either, but I delivered some updated stats to them a few weeks ago and saw her at one of the desks. I couldn't help but notice her, or, rather, her backside, since she'd bent over to adjust some cords under her desk. A rather awkward moment ensued when she stood up and caught me staring. We both blushed as I handed over the folder to her. I remember glancing down at the nameplate on her desk—April something. I can't remember her last name—an unusual name—but I'm sure her name was April, and this definitely looks like her. I couldn't forget all that blond, curly hair."

"That still doesn't explain why we're in wedding pictures together. We've never even met, and we're certainly not married."

Kenny continued to rub his chin as he turned page after page, concentration creasing his forehead, until he finally jabbed his index finger at a page. "Hey, you know what I think?" His words slowly built with dawning realization. "I think these pictures look very familiar." Yes, Michael had thought so too. "I think this is the wedding we all went to a few months back for the old man's granddaughter. Look." He pointed to a shot of the bride and groom's table in the background.

Narrowing his eyes, focusing on the small figures in the back, Michael nodded. Yes, that was it, the spoiled granddaughter's wedding, where no expense had been spared. Michael clapped a hand on Kenny's back.

"Despite the office rumors, you are brilliant, my friend. Looks to me like someone doctored those pictures and changed the lead actors. Without the actors knowing, or at least one of them."

A seething burn began under Michael's skin. He struggled to maintain the cool business composure that bolstered his reputation, but this went beyond corporate politics or boardroom etiquette. It smacked of meddling and downright taking control.

Someone was messing with him, and he didn't like it.

Anyone who knew him knew he was not the marrying kind. Oh, he had nothing against marriage—for other people. Just not him. He liked his single life. He liked his posh, state-of-the-art condo, his carefully structured schedule, his freedom to come and go as he pleased. He'd worked all his life to get to this height in his career. Marriage would only complicate all that. He was not marrying material. Not now, not ever.

"Web Works, huh?" Michael cleared his throat and straightened his tie. "Well, maybe I'll just pay them a visit and see what Miss Curly Hair has to say."

April fumbled with her mouse cable for the umpteenth time. The stupid thing had a way of getting caught in the jumble of wires that snaked around the back of her computer, forcing her to once again rearrange the clutter of discs and flash drives around her workspace.

Of course, if she took the time to organize the farmed-out projects the freelancers dumped on her haphazard desk every week, maybe this ongoing problem wouldn't catch her off guard. But organization wasn't one of her strong points. Who had the time or the patience? She managed to find things when she needed them despite herself. Her concentration was better spent on the detail-oriented work of a graphic designer. Something she was good at, thank you very much.

After untangling the mouse cord and making a mental note to ask Tim for a wireless, she sat down in her creaky chair and yawned with the intensity of a lunch-deprived, overworked computer geek. She loved her job, but at times she wondered if there was life after Web design. It wouldn't surprise her if she began dreaming in HTML code.

Shaking that scary image from her head, she lazily glanced up and for a second thought she *was* dreaming. A man in a neatly starched white shirt, cuffs secured with bulky gold cuff links, peered in the glass window from the hallway as though looking for someone. When his eyes locked on hers, she knew that trouble had come a-calling.

It's him!

April struggled to drain the surprise from her face but couldn't stop the heated flush burning deeper into her cheeks.

Oh, Lord, he's even better-looking up close.

In an effort to look innocent as well as to feign indifference, she turned back to her screen and mouse.

It's just a coincidence. He's not coming in.

The door opened, and the resulting swirl of cool air awakened every nerve ending that only minutes before had threatened to fall asleep. No, that wasn't true. *He* had awakened them. The man she'd seen only from a distance in the lobby food court. The man whose pictures she'd happened upon in her file photos. The man who looked as though he belonged on one of her mother's soap operas, with the glamorous life of a corporate whiz to match.

And here he was, walking into her office, toward her desk, and—God help her—stopping in front of her. How was she going to get out of this?

"Excuse me, you're April, right?"

How did he know her name? She turned her head. *Oh, right,* she chastised herself as her eyes followed his to her nameplate.

"Yes. Can I help you with something?"

Stay cool.

His dark eyes silently searched her face. He took in every part of it, starting with her hair, then working his way down until his gaze settled upon her mouth. She tightened her lips, afraid they might quiver with the heated sensation his stare ignited. She had no idea how long they looked at each other, but it seemed an eternity.

Was he testing her? Did he expect her to burst into tears and admit her guilt?

He suddenly blinked away the mesmerized glare and snapped to attention with a determined look. April's insides tightened, waiting for the question that would expose her foolish act.

He fumbled with a large manila envelope, impatiently looking around for a place to set it down. April's shaking hands obliged him by pushing aside a lopsided pile on her desk, only to upset another pile, sending a CD jewel case clattering to the floor just as he stepped forward.

The crunch of plastic overpowered her gasp but not his choking exclamation when he glanced down and realized what he'd done. His genuine distress—or disbelief—at clumsily crushing the case deepened a vertical line in his forehead, which pointed downward to his perfect nose and even farther to his perfect mouth. She focused on his lips rather than risk the danger of his eyes.

But when he spoke, her gaze rose to meet his pained expression, eyes searching for forgiveness. "Oh, I'm so sorry. I wasn't watching . . ."

Looking away, April casually waved. "It's okay." It wasn't. "It's nothing important." It was.

He set the heavy envelope down and bent to pick up the crushed case. "I'm afraid this won't be much good to you," he said, handing over the blood and sweat of a project she'd worked on for two months and more hours than she cared to add up.

"No problem. I have a copy." On her hard drive only, and she'd better remember to save it as soon as Prince Charming left!

He seemed relieved. "That's good, because I don't know how I'd make it up to you."

"No problem. Really." Her fingers began to cramp. She didn't realize she'd been clenching her fists, waiting for whatever punishment came her way. Why didn't he just say what he wanted and be done with it? Yes, she'd created the wedding album. Yes, she'd used his photo. Yes, she was a fool for losing track of it at the restaurant that night.

"Listen, the reason I'm here . . ."

Here it comes.

Just then the door opened, and April's boss, Tim Houghton, came sauntering back from his extended lunch. Why couldn't he have come back five minutes earlier? She would've been downstairs enjoying a relaxing lunch, free from her interrogator. But, no, Tim had a way of sniffing out ways to make her life more miserable, if that were even possible. Good thing she liked him.

All three looked at one another with expectation, but no one spoke.

Finally, Tim cocked his head. "Michael, right? From upstairs—Gellar Investments?" He extended his hand.

Confused, Michael returned the offered shake and nodded. "Yes, Michael Goode."

"Tim Houghton. We met at Cindy's wedding. Cindy—your boss' granddaughter. I was one of the photographers. Mr. Gellar asked me to take pictures to post online for all his out-of-town relatives and friends."

Like the moment when dawn becomes day, April swore she saw a cloud of haze lift from Michael's face and evaporate before her eyes. Trouble was, his now-clear eyes pierced her own with a sharpness she felt at the bottom of her stomach. Gone was the uncertainty, the question, the apology. In its place were pure conviction and a touch of self-satisfaction.

He knew.

Oh, Lord, someone must've found the album, and now he knew. If she hadn't been so scatterbrained that night with the girls at Over The Edge, she wouldn't have lost it, and she wouldn't be sitting there trying to come up with a darn good explanation or worrying about the layers of armor that had just been pierced.

How could she be so lame as to pull a stunt like that? It'd been a moment of weakness after the last of her friends became engaged. Tim's wedding shots had fired up her self-pity, and she'd wanted to see herself as a bride once and for all. Since Stan, her former almost-fiancé, had stripped that dream away long ago, she'd lost confidence in ever finding true love. Or at least finding it again.

Tim looked from one to the other again. "Uh, you already know April?"

With a mischievous lift of one eyebrow, Michael replied crisply, "No, I just stepped in, and we unfortunately didn't get as far as a formal introduction, but I feel as if I know her already." The twinkle in his dark brown eyes made her dizzy with dread. He sent a knowing glance toward the broken CD case. "I'm afraid our meeting came to a crashing halt."

"Well, then, Michael Goode, this is my associate, April Vaillancourt."

Michael's amused gaze only added to her discomfort. Maybe she should just get up and go to lunch, leave the good old boys to chat up a storm without her.

"Vaillancourt? How French. Do you speak it?"

She detested the traitorous blush on her unforgiving fair complexion. "No, I'm afraid the only thing French about me is the name." She reached for the ringing phone, but Tim waved her off and took the incoming call.

"Too bad," Michael whispered. "Maybe we could take in a French restaurant sometime, where I can dazzle you with my vast knowledge of French cuisine."

His smooth-as-glass invitation slid off his practiced tongue without the slightest effort. Just like Silver-Tongue Stan. Was that a prerequisite for corporate climbers? Say anything to make yourself look good and get what you want? She shuddered at the thought of getting involved with someone like that again.

She narrowed her eyes at Michael, knowing the scoundrel was baiting her. She sensed it down to her toenails.

"That's very appealing, but the tyrant here"—April nodded in Tim's direction—"keeps me working past my bedtime."

"But you have to eat. Everyone does sooner or later."

She laughed. "Ever hear of vending machines and delivery service?"

Michael's face looked strained for a moment, as though she hadn't answered as expected; then he shifted uneasily—or impatiently. "Yes, but I only resort to them in extreme emergencies."

With a flippant wave, April countered, "Well, every day there's an emergency around here. Guess we're not as sophisticated as Gellar Investments."

Her wave continued to include their less than stellar surroundings: metal desks, worn chairs, mismatched filing cabinets, and file folders everywhere. Yet their computers tipped the scale in the other direction. Tim spared no expense when it came to the top-of-the-line design equipment.

Michael's easy smile reappeared in a slow, upturned curve, and he glanced from Tim to April. "Yes, well, I see that you're very busy, so I won't take up any more of your time." He turned to go.

Just then, Tim hung up from his phone call. "Was there something you came down for?" he asked, obviously confused by the whole encounter.

A long moment of hesitation played out while Michael sized up the two anticipatory faces. "Just curious," he finally said, reaching for his large envelope. "I thought I'd see where our wonderful Web service comes from."

She noticed no wedding band on the outstretched hand. Not surprising. Like Stan, he probably had no time for commitments. Too busy conquering the world. Figures that she'd make the same mistake for her make-believe groom as she did for her almost-was groom.

Tim bubbled at the compliment. "Well, stay, and let me show you around, show you some of the other projects we're working on."

No, Tim, no! Let him go before I have a panic attack and break into dry heaves.

"I'll take a rain check on that. When we all have more time, maybe, I'd love to see exactly how photos and graphics are manipulated. It's a fascinating art."

Yep, he knows. He's toying with me to see if I'll break.

"Sure, anytime." Tim escorted Michael to the entrance. "Our door is always open. We work 'cause the Web Works."

Michael turned a curious gaze at Tim, as though uncertain of the joke, then laughed. "Catchy. Very good." Then, without even glancing back, he added, "Nice meeting you, April."

Once again the door whooshed, and he was gone. The room gradually stilled. Her heart rate slowed. The earth resumed rotation on its slightly tilted axis.

Thank God.

"What in the world was that all about?" Tim's high-pitched question sent her peace and quiet scrambling for cover. She should've known her longtime friend would pick up on the tension. She loved working with Tim, but sometimes she wished he didn't know her quite so well.

April occupied herself shuffling discs at her desk, avoiding Tim's eyes. "You're asking me? I'm not the one he was talking to."

"I meant, what was that static charge in the air when I walked in? You two looked as though you were digging in for a face-off. What'd I miss?"

"Nothing, he came in with . . ." She paused, reaching for her bottle of water. "He looked like he wanted to show me whatever was in the big envelope, but then he stepped on this." She lifted the crackled plastic case. "And then you walked in. He seemed to change his mind after you said you knew him from the wedding."

She unscrewed the cap of her bottle and thought about the heavy thud when he'd put the large envelope down. Could it have been the album?

A long sip of water didn't even come close to extinguishing that burning question. It was all she could think about—that and his dark eyes and dimpled smile. She'd noticed the one-sided dimple in the photos, even toyed with the idea of graphically removing it to even out the smile.

But she hadn't. She'd left it in, wondering what it would be like to run her finger over it as he smiled down at her.

Tim adjusted his glasses. "Well, all I know is, you'd better be careful. He works for one of our biggest clients. The last thing we need is an enemy at Gellar."

Sorry, Tim, you're way too late for that.

Chapter Two

At a corner table in the brightly lit food court, Michael drummed his fingers atop the thick envelope with the cursed wedding album inside, the hollow thump marking time with his pounding heart.

What had just happened up there? He'd headed to Web Works determined to get to the bottom of the problem. But some mysterious, unseen force seemed to have hijacked his clear-cut mission.

Instead, he'd fumbled—no, *stumbled* was more like it—in a most uncharacteristically clumsy way and found himself nearly panting at the intriguing woman with the hypnotizing eyes and endless blond curls.

The cracking sound of the plastic case he'd stepped on practically ridiculed his usually impenetrable, collected persona as though it too had just cracked. And when he'd looked up into April's alluring eyes, she'd appeared indifferent, unconcerned, coolly turning back to her work.

Not the normal reaction he got from women, much to his discontent.

Without exception, one look from his piercing, direct gaze always rendered women speechless and pliable to his whim. But this one, with her wild curls and indirect glances, gave him pause. Her clear blue eyes had smiled at him, almost mockingly, yet something else in those eyes hinted at her own unsettled state when she avoided his gaze.

Deceit? Fear?

Without a doubt, she knew who he was the minute he'd walked in, but had she any idea *why* he was there? If he'd asked her point-

14

blank about the album before Tim Houghton walked in, as he'd intended, would she have answered him honestly?

On the other hand, could it have been Tim's dirty deed? He did take the pictures, after all, and knew that Michael had been at the wedding. But if Tim had actually orchestrated this farce, Michael doubted he'd be so eager to reintroduce himself and make a point of talking about the wedding.

No, April was the one with the guilty look, the one he needed to focus on.

Known as a man of action who always accomplished what he set out to do, Michael admitted he'd faltered this time. But his father had taught him to never give up on a goal. Step back, reassess the situation, and then move forward with a revised plan. That's what had made him who he was today: a man from a single-parent family of limited means turned high-powered financial whiz. He'd made his father proud.

Whatever had changed the dynamics of his objective toward April, he'd instinctively refrained from asking her questions about the album until he got a better grasp of the situation. Experience had taught him to be thorough, research the opponent, and know his or her faults. More important, he liked the idea of finding out exactly *who* this April Vaillancourt was. Why they were in a wedding album together would follow later.

As though summoned by his subconscious, the lovely blond sailed into the food court, hell-bent on the burger stand, her curls bouncing to her unladylike gait.

Michael glanced down at her feet, which shuffled along in green suede clogs, and chuckled to himself. Green clogs, blue jeans, and a gauze tunic-style top, which camouflaged any hint of a feminine shape. Nothing matched, everything looked borrowed, and the fit didn't seem to matter.

He could only hope her talent in graphic design exceeded her taste in fashion.

Mesmerized all the same by what seemed to be an air of static electricity that surrounded her, he followed her progress along the counter, to the cashier, then to a small round table in the middle of the dining area. She lifted a covered cold drink and a paper plate with a burger and French fries from her brown plastic tray before tossing it onto a nearby refuse stand. She settled into her chair, hooked her heels onto the metal bar beneath her seat, then leaned forward and began devouring her lunch.

Michael shook his head. This was more than fate at work; it was divine intervention telling him to pick himself up, dust himself off, and stick to the agenda. After all, he was the golden boy who never failed in a mission, be it business or personal; he always got what he went after. Once he defined his goal, he merely set his sights and forged ahead. His father had taught him well.

Rising from his seat, he crossed the court, weaving in and out of the tables with renewed confidence. He wanted answers, and he was certain April Vaillancourt had them.

"Hi again."

April jumped. One foot slipped off the metal bar of her chair, and her clog thunked loudly as it hit the tile floor.

"Hi, uh, Michael."

"So, you *do* like French food." He nodded toward her fries and smiled.

She shrugged. "I suppose." The joke soared over her head and sailed into space.

"May I?" He pulled out the chair before she assented. "I was wondering . . ."

He placed the photo album in front of him on the small table, but the weight shifted the table just enough to unsettle her plate of fries, which nudged the manila envelope. A glob of ketchup slid to the side and stained the once-clean envelope like freshly drawn blood. They both reached for the napkin dispenser in a hasty effort to stop the bleeding but instantly retracted as their hands touched in a moment of heated hesitation.

"It seems," he noted, "I'm all thumbs and left feet when I'm around you."

"Really?" she mumbled with a decided lack of interest after chewing a mouthful of fries. "I hadn't noticed."

"I still feel bad about stepping on that jewel case. Totally out of character for me."

"So normally you're very put-together and completely charming."

"Completely. But then, you already knew that, right?"

"I did? How would I know that? We just met." She stuffed two more fries into her mouth and quickly grabbed for her drink.

"I'm not so sure about that." He nudged the envelope with the back of his hand, coaxing it aside. Wide-eyed, her gaze followed the movement. "Something tells me either we've met before or we've been somewhere at the same time."

He watched April's full lips circle the straw tightly, then her cheeks hollow as she rapidly sucked in the soda and swallowed, choking back a tiny cough from her vigorous intake. Her eyes, riveted on the envelope, teared as the carbonation bubbled its way up her nose. She *knew* what was in there.

"Oh, I don't think so. I would've remembered, uh, someone like you."

"Someone like me? Meaning?"

She shrugged. "You know, smooth, sharp dresser, in command of himself."

"Why, thank you. But clothes don't necessarily tell you everything about a person."

The table shook as her knee bounced beneath it. He watched her cup do a slow slide in its moisture ring. She looked about to respond, then chomped down on another bite of her burger instead. Her unsettled demeanor only strengthened his resolve.

"No, I'm sure we know each other from somewhere. I never forget a face." He rested a hand on the album and tapped a finger in a thoughtful gesture. "Did you go to the Gellar Christmas reception?"

"No, I don't work for Gellar. Why would I go there?"

"They invite key vendors and reps. I thought you might've come with Tim."

"No, I didn't." She continued eating, but her clear blue eyes shifted repeatedly from her food to the album under his hand.

"What about the wedding?"

April choked hard, her lashes batting back tears, as she brushed aside her drink to reach for a napkin. Covering her mouth, she took some deep breaths between coughs while cautiously eyeing Michael's reaction.

"Are you okay?" he asked, suppressing amusement at his expert marksmanship. She nodded and waved the napkin before another cough shook her. "I think you were trying to eat too fast. Here."

He handed her the drink, which she obligingly took. After several minutes of short sips and shorter coughs, she finally caught her breath and sighed.

"Okay now?"

"Yes." Her voice was choppy from the physical strain. "You're right. I *was* eating too fast, because I have to get back to work." She rose. "I'll see you around." And she was off.

Startled by her sudden exit, Michael hastened to his feet, groping for the manila envelope. But his fingertips sank into the wet glob of ketchup, stopping him in his tracks. He cursed under his breath, then grabbed April's discarded napkin to mop the nasty smear. He checked his shirt to make sure nothing had splattered on his clean white sleeve.

With another muttered curse, he hurried after April and caught up with her just outside the swinging door.

"You mean to tell me you only get ten minutes for lunch?"

"No, I just have a tight schedule today. I need to finish a project before five." Her shoes clopped down the foyer hall until she stopped at the elevators.

Michael scrambled for something to say. He still hadn't broached the matter of the album. But just the mention of a wedding had sent her reeling and convinced him she knew all the details of the photos. What he didn't know was why and how the collection had ended up in a public restaurant.

Shaking his head, he glanced down at the blond locks before him. A tropical scent wafted up to meet his nose, enticing him to inhale deeply. She was at least a head shorter than he, not quite petite but trim with some natural curves. At least the ones he saw move against the tunic when she walked.

Preceded by a *ding,* the elevator doors slid open, and Michael sighed resignedly as he noticed a man wearing a dirty repairman's uniform inside. When April stepped in, the man smiled at her—a little too suggestively for Michael's liking. He purposely stepped to the back of the elevator, between April and the repairman, and when the man peered around to stare at April, Michael shot him his best "hands off" glare. Edging closer to her, he again caught a hint of that delicious scent.

The car stopped two floors up, and the man got out. As soon as the doors closed again, April folded her arms and cleared her throat.

"You can step away now."

"Are you asking me or telling me?"

She hesitated a second. "I'm suggesting there's no need for your proximity."

"Well, some other lecherous person might get on, and I'd hate to see you unprotected."

She turned to him, her eyes fiery, her nostrils flared. "I ride this elevator every day, and I've always felt perfectly safe. Until now."

Feigning shock, he put a hand to his chest. "Are you suggesting I make you feel unsafe? I had only your best interests in mind. I thought if he saw us as a couple, you know, you being spoken for, he wouldn't bother you. It seemed to work. Of course, with your chilly reaction and lack of response to me, he probably thought we were married."

April opened her mouth wide, but no words came out. He knew he'd hit on the one thing to keep her from lashing back with an acidic remark. Just then the elevator stopped, the doors opened at her floor, and all he saw was that cute little pink tongue inside her dark, moist mouth rimmed by a dainty upper lip and a full lower one.

Her scent still surrounded him, and her curls waved in the gentle brush of air from the open doors. She was the most tempting thing he'd seen in a long time, and he had her complete attention following his mention of marriage.

Ah, yes, a sensitive topic with her.

When still she said nothing and her open lips invited him closer, without thinking he moved forward and dropped a kiss onto her unsuspecting mouth. She tasted like salt from the fries and sweet from the ketchup.

With a self-satisfied smile, he waited for her response, something that said she'd enjoyed it. Instead, she grabbed the album out of his hand and unceremoniously dropped it on his foot. As he yelled and hopped—and nearly bit his tongue off—she dashed out the doors just before they closed and the car continued on its way.

Michael checked his watch so he'd know exactly what time he'd lost his sanity.

April rushed through the office, ignored Tim's shouted question about some layout, and headed directly for the restroom at the back.

She had to see what her face looked like after what she'd just been through.

A kiss! My God, he'd kissed her in the elevator, without warning, without provocation, and despite her attempts to be rid of him! What kind of man would do such a thing?

An arrogant, self-assured, pompous egomaniac, that's who. She knew the type. She'd been engaged to one! And where had it gotten her? Eight years down the bumpy road of her life with no one to sleep near or come home to. Her heart remained as empty as Stan's promises had been.

Well, she wouldn't let this Michael Goode make any promises. He might be good-looking and sexy as all get out, but she had experience on her side. She knew how to avoid the bait.

Plainly the man had baited her, yet she couldn't be sure. If he'd just out-and-out accused her, she might've buckled under the pressure and blurted out her insane scheme. Instead, he'd just made subtle hints, suggestions, waiting for her to trip up and expose her best-ever April Fool's joke.

Yes, she'd gotten the girls good with that one. Their yearly ritual of an April Fool's dinner—she being the original instigator—had been preceded by weeks of agonizing melancholy now that her friend Christine had gotten engaged.

April was the last unattached friend in the famous foursome from high school. More and more their talks centered around babies, husbands, early dinners, quiet weekends. April often found herself cringing at the unfamiliar topics yet wishing she had a man to share the same with.

Where had all the good men gone?

So when she'd stumbled upon Tim's wedding photos file while searching their server for some clip art, the harebrained scheme had begun to germinate. Curious, April had browsed through them, imagining herself as the bride and getting whimsically wrapped up in the glamour of a big wedding—like the one she might've had with Stan if his dreams hadn't taken a different path.

Before she knew it, she'd cut, pasted, and edited a whole new set of wedding pictures. Using her own photos from her recent vacation file, it'd been so easy to substitute herself as the radiant bride and Michael Goode as the handsome groom. When she completed the fantasy by creating the album, she knew it would make a great April Fool's joke for the girls' night out.

And it did. They'd passed the album around the table, chuckling and pointing with *oohs* and *ahs* at the beautiful wedding scenes and congratulating her for her Photoshop skills. Somewhere between the laughter and the nonstop four-way conversations, April forgot about and lost track of the album. Now she faced this living nightmare.

A loud knock on the door startled her. "April, you've got a call."

She blinked away the visions in her head, then splashed some cool water onto her face. "I'll be right there." She quickly dried off, tugged a few curls from her face, and licked her lips.

She still couldn't believe he'd kissed her, but what did she expect from this smooth type of operator—lady-killer, womanizer, the type who took rather than gave? And he'd taken without any encouragement from her. In fact, she'd gone out of her way to get away from him.

But the kiss had stunned her, a taste of fantasy from her vivid imaginings on the few occasions she'd seen Michael in the food court over the past year. Not that he'd ever noticed her. But she'd noticed him, with his gravitational dimpled smile that set her heart to melting. That's why she'd chosen him from those wedding pictures to be her groom. She'd liked the idea of getting lost in that dimple.

So why did you go and drop that heavy envelope on his foot?

She shook her head. It was either that or she would've slapped his face like a heroine in an old movie. Worst of all, something deep inside had told her that that envelope held the source of her discontent—the wedding album. Ironic that she'd chosen to attack him with it.

With a quick head slap, she glared wide-eyed at herself in the mirror. *Why didn't you take it and run?* She shook her head in disbelief and stepped out of the restroom to answer her call.

Michael tapped his pen against the dark green desk pad while shouldering the phone against his ear. What was she doing? He'd seen for himself that the Web Works office wasn't that big. If she'd just stepped away from her desk, what was taking her so long to get back? Maybe she got lost in all the clutter. He shuddered at the impossibility of working under such conditions.

He thought about hanging up and going down to confront April Vaillancourt once and for all. But, flexing his still-throbbing foot, he thought better of it. At least for now. He needed some kind of game plan, a strategy that would allow him to get to know the mystery bride while figuring out how it had all happened. After all, he had no proof she was the culprit. Conceivably, someone else, even Tim, could've edited the photos as a joke.

But why? He didn't know either of them. What would be the point of such a prank?

"Hello, this is April."

Pulled from his reverie, Michael sat up straighter and banged his sore foot against the heavy wood desk leg. A curse disguised as a grunt was all he could manage until the pain subsided.

"Excuse me? Who's calling?" April's cautious business voice warned him she was busy.

"Sorry, I bumped my sore foot. This is Michael, Michael Goode from Gellar Investments."

"Oh," was all she said while her silence told him to get lost.

"Listen, I want to apologize for that rude . . . moment in the elevator. I don't know what came over me. I've been a little out of sorts lately—you know, corporate pressures and all." He laid the

Goode charm on thick, then waited for a placating assurance from her, but none came. "Anyway, that's still no reason for my action, and I'd like to make it up to you. Perhaps that dinner we talked about—"

"No."

Michael gripped his pen. "Well, I see you gave that a lot of thought. If you don't like French, we could do Italian or Chinese or—"

"No."

He tossed the pen aside. "You aren't going to make this easy, are you? If I promise to stay at least an arm's length from your lips at all times—"

"No."

He sat forward and braced both elbows on the desk as though she could see his determination. "I think it's the least you can do for me."

"What?"

At last she'd said something besides no. "You *did* drop that heavy package on my foot, and now I have to limp to my next meeting with my top client. It could be quite distracting. Might hurt my business. Do you want that on your conscience?"

"I—I don't like being cornered."

"I didn't corner you. I was merely trying to protect you."

"Protect me? Was my mouth in danger?" She'd lowered her voice to a sultry whisper, more than likely to keep Tim from hearing.

He chuckled. "Okay, I deserved that. It just seemed the right thing to do at the time. My judgment was off. Forgive me." Women couldn't resist self-defeat.

"I'll say."

"Then let's try again. Let's pretend none of that happened and have a nice, quiet, get-to-know-you dinner. Anywhere you'd like."

When she didn't answer right away, he began to smile to himself. Smooth as always.

"I don't think so. I need to get back to work."

"I didn't mean now. I meant—" *Click.* She hung up.

She hung up!

His frustration at an all-time high, Michael slammed the phone down, shoved back his chair, and elevated his sore foot on the desk. He'd never get to the bottom of this wedding-album thing if he couldn't even see her.

Rocking his chair in time with his agitated pulse, he cursed at himself for not asking her straight out. He should've produced the album and forced her to explain it.

But deep down he almost didn't want to know the truth. This mystery, this chase, was much more fun. More fun than he'd had in a long time. Sheila, his last love interest, had nearly bored him to death. She'd yessed everything he said, hung on to his arm wherever they walked, and cried when he showed up with flowers or candy. So predictable. Totally uninteresting.

Since then, he'd sunk himself into his work and only dated occasionally, mostly when a business function required an appearance as a couple. That had made for a long dry spell of over nine months, which had also added to the mystery of his long weekend away, at least as far as Kenny Gellar was concerned.

Speaking of which, he needed to talk to that freeloader.

Gently lowering his foot, Michael sat forward again and reached for the phone. "Kenny, got a minute?"

Within seconds his associate shuffled into his office. "What's up?" His attention went to the package on the desk. "Didn't you find her?"

"Yes, I, uh, I never got around to asking her."

Kenny closed the door quickly. "You're kidding. Mr. Get-to-the-point? Why not? What happened?"

"Look, I can't answer that right now. I'm working on it. In the meantime, I have to ask you something. What did you think of that notice about your uncle retiring next April? Do you think he'll really do it this time? And who do you think he'll name CEO?"

Kenny made himself comfortable in one of the big leather chairs in front of Michael's desk, his tented fingers before him.

"Yes, I think he's serious this time, but I think the CEO position is up for grabs. He's given himself plenty of time, almost a full year, to observe and choose carefully. He'll probably instigate in-house fighting and see who comes out the victor. He's always had a weird sense of competition. You know, 'may the best man win.'"

"What about you? Will you fight for it?"

"Me? Nah, I don't need those headaches. I'm happy doing what I do. My wife brings in a decent salary as a legal secretary, and I see no need to complicate my life for the sake of a title and pay raise."

"Then who do you think he'll tap? Or will he bring in new blood?"

"Michael, why are you asking me this? I think it's obvious you're the only sane choice. You have the brains, the ambition, the personality. You've been the fuel fanning this corporate flame for the last few years. I can only think of one thing you have against you."

"What's that?"

"You're single. You know how he is about stability and family. My God, look at the wedding he threw for his granddaughter. Her parents were perfectly willing to pay for a nice, not overly extravagant wedding. But Uncle Howard wanted nothing but the best for his only grandchild."

"But what's that got to do with my promotion?"

"See, in his eyes, if you're single, you're not stable. I mean, you could just pick up and leave anytime you wanted. What's to stop you from taking a job at another company, in another state? He can't compete with that, and then he'd be right back to finding a successor. There's nothing tying you down here."

Michael averted his gaze. So true, more than Kenny knew. That weekend away had been his fact-finding mission for another job. He'd only declined the offer because it meant a lateral move rather than upward, and the slight raise didn't compensate for the connections he'd made and the groundwork he'd laid at Gellar Investments.

"But you don't think Howard would promote me if I remain single."

"I don't presume to read his mind. I just know his thoughts on family values and their importance to a career man. He wants someone at the helm who'll care about the company, about its growth. Someone who'll stick with it as a lifelong commitment. Just like marriage."

Kenny's silly grin rattled Michael. Why did he get the feeling he was being set up?

"Well, I'm not getting married anytime soon, so I guess I'll just have to take my chances."

"Too bad." Kenny got up, then nodded to the envelope on Michael's desk. "Course, there are some people who already think you're married. Shelley, me . . ."

Michael narrowed his eyes, warning Kenny to keep quiet. "You know this is a hoax. I'm the ultimate confirmed bachelor."

"So you say." With a deep, throaty laugh, Kenny exited humming, "Here Comes the Bride."

"Fool," Michael muttered. If he kept that up, everyone in the office would start thinking . . .

Like a finger in an electrical socket, Michael jolted at the thought. What if they *did* start thinking? What if the old man got wind of the "marriage"? Michael would only have to perpetrate the rumor until a successor was named. Preferably him. Could he pull it off?

Maybe, just maybe, with a little cooperation.

Chapter Three

The clock read seven thirty, but it felt more like midnight to April. She'd been working on the same Web site since ten that morning with barely a break.

Well, she'd had a few, but they'd all seemed to revolve around that full-of-himself Michael Goode, who was siphoning off way too much of her concentration.

She'd have to be very careful not to run into him in the food court again, because who knew how long she could maintain the poker face? Even if all evidence indicated he knew about the album, she couldn't just blurt it out. She had to wait for him to ask. And when he did, she'd spill like a gutted fish.

Glancing over at Tim, who glared at his screen like an enemy in a duel, she decided she'd had enough. All creativity had ceased hours ago.

"Tim, I'm heading out. My eyes can't focus anymore."

"Sure." He waved. "I'll see you in the morning."

She loved the working relationship between them. They'd been friends long before Tim became her boss, so she never felt like just an employee. Tim treated her as an equal, with great respect for her creativity and talent. She never regretted leaving her old job to become a part of this dynamic duo called Web Works.

April shut down her computer, slipped her backup flash drive into her purse, and headed for the coatrack in the back. But something at the door caught her eye—a delivery man with a vase of colorful flowers stood reading the name on the door across the hallway. He finally turned to Web Works and looked relieved when he pushed the door and it opened.

"Hi." He smiled wanly. "Delivery for April Valcourt?"

"Vaillancourt," April sighed. No one ever got her name right. "That's me."

"Thank goodness. Sorry it's so late. There was a mix-up on the last-minute order." He tipped his baseball hat and rushed out as though he'd just escaped losing his job.

Tired and confused, April frowned at the vase of assorted cut flowers, unsure what to do with them. Who would send her flowers, and why? She set them down near her computer, then thought better of it, remembering the fate of the CD case earlier. The last thing she needed was an accidental spill to fry her equipment.

Since every counter in the place had some kind of scanner, printer, computer, camera, or docking station, she had little choice but to unload the vase on the set of filing cabinets between her and Tim's desks. With one hand she coaxed a pile of magazines and mail folders to one side, barely making enough room for the heavy glass vase. She frowned at the odd sight of age-old clutter sprouting flowers.

"Okay if I leave these here?"

"Sure," Tim answered without looking away from his screen. But as she opened the small white envelope attached, he exclaimed, "Where did those come from?"

"The Flower Pot on the East Side."

"I mean, who sent them?"

She read the card and tightened her lips. "Michael Goode, Gellar Investments."

If her mother, the hopeless romantic, had been there, she might have swooned. But then, her mother still held out hope that Stan would come back to sweep April off her feet.

"Really?" He turned in his chair and cast a frown similar to hers at the unusual sight of flowers on their ancient filing cabinets. He nudged his glasses a notch higher. "What exactly were you two doing while I was at lunch?"

"Get real, Tim. He's got a guilty conscience, that's all, and he thinks this will smooth things over."

"But from the tone of your voice, it won't, right? Geez, April, all he did was step on your CD case. Give the guy a break."

She rolled her eyes and reached for her coat. "Yeah, a CD case. No big thing." She'd never hear the end of it if Tim knew about the kiss, the real reason for Michael's guilty conscience. "I'll see you tomorrow."

"Hey, don't you want to take the flowers home?"

"Nope," she called back without turning. "You can if you want." She walked out of the office, her clogs echoing heavily in the deserted, tile-lined hall.

Taking the flowers home would only remind her what a horrible day this had been and what a pickle she'd gotten herself into. If only she hadn't made that stupid wedding album, none of this would've happened.

Of course, she was only speculating here. She had no real proof that Michael Goode knew about the album. She had no way of knowing if that's what had been in the big envelope. It could all be a coincidence, his stopping by, his placing the envelope within her reach, his unsettling glances. None of it meant he knew. If he did, why hadn't he just said so or confronted her with the evidence?

What was he waiting for?

And then there was that kiss. She shivered just thinking about it. Even her toes remembered the tingling sensation of his bold mouth on hers.

Okay, so maybe the whole day hadn't been quite so horrible, but she still didn't want to be reminded of it, or him. Corporate climbers were not on her A-list of men to attract. She'd done her time as the woman in waiting while Stan hopped from city to city with each promotion. His promises of a life together soon fell flat, along with her dream of marriage.

Aside from all that, Michael Goode was way out of her league. Her accidental wardrobe was no match for his exquisitely tailored suits and shirts. And despite his offer, French cuisine would be wasted on her. She was a pizza and burger kind of gal. She made enough money to pay her rent, put gas in her car, and enjoy a movie now and again. Fancy clothes and restaurants never entered the picture.

Even without all that against her, how could she face him after what she'd done? At the time it'd seemed like the funniest and best April Fool's joke. Now it just reeked of a pathetic school-girl's longing.

She sighed as she pressed the elevator button. Make-believe or real, marriage didn't appear to be anywhere in her future.

The next morning a package addressed to April arrived at the Web Works office by overnight delivery. Intrigued, she tore open the outer carton and lifted out a gold-foil-covered box accompanied by the most delectable sweet scent of chocolate.

Godiva.

From Michael, who else? The rat knew which buttons to push. Her mother would definitely be swooning now. What woman could resist chocolate?

She could, if accepting it meant swallowing her pride. She walked the box over to Tim's desk.

"Here, have some chocolate."

Tim's eyes widened when he saw the shiny brown delights inside. "Oh, man, these are awesome." He popped one into his mouth and picked another to sit by him for all of two minutes.

April dropped the box atop some file folders by his elbow. "You can keep them over here."

"What, are you kidding? What'd I do to deserve this?"

"Nothing. It's just your lucky day."

With a painfully screwed-up look on his face, he scrutinized her from head to toe. "Are you okay? You look a little . . . funny."

That's what came of working with Tim all these years—he knew her too well. He knew her moods too, and when she fell into a foul one, he gave her a wide berth.

April laughed and went back to her desk. "Yes, now leave me alone. I want to finish this design today."

And forget about Michael Goode.

The hours slipped by. As lunchtime approached, her grumbling stomach suggested she run downstairs for a quick bite, but she fought the urge and the risk of a chance encounter with Michael. Instead she convinced Tim to go out for sandwiches, her treat.

Her energy replenished, she dove back into her work and barely paid attention when the phone rang. Tim fielded the call, agreed with the caller's request, then rose after he hung up.

"I have to go upstairs. Gellar's marketing director wants to go over some statistics from the Web site."

"'Kay," she mumbled, clicking away with her mouse.

Finally, the design was taking shape, but it needed one more thing, something unique and eye-opening. She chuckled to herself at the pun on the client: what would be eye-opening to an optometrist?

"Hi."

April jumped at the sound, wondering where the voice had come from, and jumped a second time when she turned and saw it belonged to Michael Goode. Looking starched and fresh, he sauntered in, hands casually slung in his perfectly pressed pockets. He smiled just enough to deepen his dimple and capture her stare. His gaze darted about, as though he was looking for something or someone.

"Tim's not here. He had to go up—" Michael nodded, not surprised with her explanation. "Oh, you *knew* he was up there."

"Yes, I saw him in the meeting room. Marketing is really hung up on the numbers this month." He paced a small circle around the cramped two-and-a-half-person office that barely contained two people jammed in among mountains of equipment, all necessary tools of the trade. The look on his face fell somewhere between smug and a cat watching a canary.

"You don't have a lot of room around here, do you?"

"Enough. Everything we need is within our reach."

"But that doesn't leave much room for aesthetics, like decorations, flowers."

"I'm too busy to be bothered with flowers."

His face tightened. "I see."

"Yes, Michael, I received your flowers. Very pretty, but totally unnecessary."

He looked around again. "So, you took them home?"

"No, I think Tim did." She glanced over at the file cabinet to be sure. "I'm not good with plants."

Michael's eyes hardened. "And the chocolates?"

She shrugged. "I don't know what Tim did with the rest. I know he ate half of them before lunch."

He tugged an impatient hand out of his pocket and ran it through his hair. "April, I didn't send those gifts for Tim. He's not the one I'm trying to impress."

"Well, you're wasting your time trying to impress me."

"Why? Are you married?"

She opened her mouth to answer, but a frightful squeak came out. Was it just her imagination, or did every sentence, every thought of his, end with a comment about marriage? No, she didn't imagine it. He had a purpose.

"No, I—"

"Good. Then I can keep trying." The beginnings of a smile twitched at the corners of his mouth.

"I beg your pardon?"

"To impress you. You're quite a challenge. I rarely have this much difficulty with women."

"Is that what I am, a challenge?" She rose from her desk, hoping to diminish his advantage over her in height. "Because I blew you off the first time, you have to keep coming back until I succumb?"

Crossing his arms over his chest, Michael's smile widened. A wicked, arrogant smile. "*Succumb* is an awfully strong word. Think of it more in terms of negotiation."

He was playing with her again. His self-assured smile reminded her of her vulnerability and that he knew something she didn't. Or something he didn't think she knew.

"Look, I'm not in the mood for any *negotiations* right now. I have a lot of work to finish up."

"No wonder you're not married." He shrugged at the glare she shot him. "I mean, no time to find that special someone."

She'd heard that same observation dozens of times from family and friends who thought she should spend more time in search of a life partner and less on her work. Well, she didn't. Her mother had stayed at home, her job as perfect homemaker fulfilling her dreams. But April's fulfillment grew out of her talent for graphic design, which buoyed her confidence, more so because she didn't have to depend on unreliables like Stan to provide for her.

She loved her career and planned to keep it, thank you very much.

"You don't even know me, so don't presume to understand me."

"But that's the whole point. I *want* to get to know you. I *want* to understand you. But if you keep hiding behind that workaholic mask, you'll never get to meet anyone, let alone get to know them."

"Well, maybe I don't care to know you."

"Why? What've I done to you?" He suddenly leaned over her desk, dangerously close to her face. "And don't say that kiss in the elevator, because you enjoyed it as much as I did."

Her mouth slacked open. She shrank back into her chair. She felt as though he'd just sucker punched her right in the middle of her stomach. How could she answer that? He was right, as far as stolen kisses by a stranger in an elevator go.

April leaned one elbow on her armrest and rubbed her forehead tiredly. "Are you finished?"

"No. I came here to find out what I could do to make up for my rudeness and clumsiness and to find out if there's anything I can do to impress you. Obviously flowers and candy and French dining don't. I want to get to know you. What do you like, April? Teddy bears, jewelry, movies, long walks on the beach? Give me a clue."

She waited, letting him think she was about to reveal some powerful secret; then she sighed. "If you have to be told what to do, then the whole reason for doing it is negated."

He stepped back, nodded slightly, then rubbed his chin thoughtfully. Glancing around, he took another slow visual tour of the small office, taking in the papers tossed atop her desk, the pencil sharpener disguised as a football helmet, several posters from clients' advertising campaigns. He seemed to study all the details as though he'd find a clue about her in them.

Finally turning back to her, he raised an eyebrow. "Had lunch yet?"

"Yes, I'm all set."

He nodded. "Okay. I'll see ya."

Before she knew it, he left the office and left her more confused than ever. What was he after? She sensed an ulterior motive deeper than just a date. And if it had to do with the wedding album, why would he be so nice?

Shaking her head, she jumped back into her work. Tim returned an hour later mumbling about the lame meeting he'd had at Gellar.

"They could've cleared up the questions with a simple phone call. Why tie me up in a lengthy meeting?"

April frowned. *Why, indeed?* Ulterior motives at every turn.

At four o'clock a harried-looking delivery boy showed up at the door carrying the biggest bouquet of helium balloons April had ever seen. Rather than risk breaking them by squeezing in the door, he stood at the threshold keeping the balloons at bay out in the hallway.

"April Valcourt?"

"Vaillancourt. Yes, that's me."

"Where would you like these?"

Feeling like a little girl at a parade, she giggled at the sight of the brilliant colors bouncing outside the door. She didn't have to ask who sent them. She felt flattered and insulted all at once. But they really were beautiful.

"You'll have to take them back," she answered, figuring she had to go against Michael's game plan, if for no other reason than not giving him the upper hand. "There's no room in here."

The delivery boy shook his head. "I have strict instructions to be sure you got them personally."

Of course he did. And he probably got a nice tip to go along with it. That's when she noticed one clear white balloon with a small teddy bear inside. The bear had a red heart on its chest and a tiny flower in one of its paws.

"Awww, he's so cute," April cooed as she stepped closer.

Relieved, the boy thrust the bundle of strings into her hand so fast, she had no time to protest before he was gone. She gripped them tightly as the pull of the helium neared liftoff strength. Just then Tim came out of the restroom.

"What the— April, what's with all the balloons?"

"I don't know. Payback, I guess." Still holding the balloons outside the door, she looked around for a place to tie them.

"Since when does someone pay back with balloons?"

"Since Michael Goode got it into his head that he should impress me."

"Well, he sure impressed me. Those things aren't cheap. Payback for what?"

She started to tell Tim it was a personal matter, when Michael poked his dimpled face from behind the balloons. "Is it safe?"

April clamped her mouth shut. She had to pretend she hadn't been smiling. "You can wipe that smug look off your face, because they're not staying."

"It's not smug. It's pleasure. I finally found something you like."

She groaned and turned to Tim. "I'll be back. I have to get rid of these."

Michael followed her to the elevator. She was about to protest his company, but she knew she'd need his help getting the balloons into the elevator.

"You know, I could hold some of those if you'd like."

"No, thanks. You've done enough already," she quipped. She elbowed the Down button.

The doors slid open, and she used a back end approach to get in, with Michael pushing the resisting balloons. He squeezed himself in at the last moment. They stood on opposite sides of the elevator, unable to see each other for the colorful jumble of balloons between them.

"I guess my plan wasn't very well thought out, was it?"

"If you mean, did it make me happy? No. If you mean, would I be glad to have them? No. If you mean, would they make a nice centerpiece for my table? No. Three strikes, you're out."

"Darn," he mumbled. "I suppose first base is out of the question?"

April grunted. The elevator stopped at the ground level, and they had to strategically switch positions in order to exit. A few onlookers in the foyer smiled at the sight of a flustered woman laden with balloons and a self-assured man beaming at her reactions. She immediately headed for the main entrance.

"Where are you going?" he asked, picking up her pace.

She didn't answer; she just stepped out into the cool April air and looked skyward for inspiration.

"You're not going to release them, are you?"

The thought had occurred to her. But she couldn't bring herself to do it. She'd seen too many crying children at parades and parks with little hands stretched upward as their beautiful balloons soared beyond their reach, out of sight. If she let go, a part of her would cry out too.

And then she saw the sign: WaterFire tonight in downtown Providence, a festive occasion for this Renaissance City, with fires and music and walks along the river. While the fires on the river wouldn't be lit until dusk, she knew people—families—would be milling about preparing for the spectacle. What better place to spread the wealth?

With a quick turn, she headed down the street until she came to Memorial Boulevard. Crossing over, she made a direct beeline for Waterplace Park, where people lounged on the grass, pedestrians and kids on Rollerblades moved along the pavement, and all sorts of activity sprang up around the edges.

April found a stone bench and sat, doing her best to keep the balloons between her and Michael. He paced around the bench for a few minutes until his curiosity got the better of him.

"Why are you sitting here?"

Just then a couple approached with a little girl sporting a thick blond ponytail. "Mommy, can I get a balloon?" she pleaded excitedly.

April stood and smiled. "What's your favorite color?"

"Blue!"

"Here you go, one blue balloon, just for you. But let your mommy tie it around your wrist."

The father sheepishly dug into his pocket. "How much?"

Waving her free hand, April refused. "Oh, no, it's my pleasure."

The couple looked at each other blankly, thanked April, and walked away.

Shortly, another couple with a boy in a stroller came along. He reached out and pointed happily. "B'loon!"

April smiled and handed a purple one to the mother, who secured it to the stroller. They, too, left confused by the free-balloon vendor. April giggled. This was more fun than she'd thought.

The next family that came by had two tykes, and Michael happily assisted handing over the strings, securing one to a chubby wrist. He caught April's eyes as she glanced appreciatively at him, and he shot back with a wink. She looked away, but a tight sensation rose in her chest.

He'd gotten to her. Yes, he had.

It only took another fifteen minutes before all the balloons were gone, all but the white one. "Well, I guess that's it," April sighed, moving toward the river bridge to watch the lighting of the fires.

"What about the teddy bear? You aren't giving him away?" Michael matched his steps with hers.

Drat. She couldn't hide her weakness. "No, I thought I'd keep this one."

"So, you really do like it, huh?"

She really did. She edged her way into the last remaining open spot on the bridge and leaned on the cool stonework to look down-river.

"It'll be a reminder of how happy we made all those kids. The fun sort of took the edge off the aggravation."

He managed to squeeze in next to her, excusing himself to a couple on the other side that wasn't about to give up their prime viewing slot.

"Phew, then you're not mad at me anymore."

"Oh, I don't know if I'd go that far, but you did make a grand effort to redeem yourself." He'd seemed to genuinely enjoy treating those kids, and he'd touched the kid in her with the whole balloon idea.

He glanced at her out of the corner of his eye. "Good. That makes the rest of this a whole lot easier."

April stopped smiling and stared directly at him. "The rest? You mean there's more?"

He cleared his throat and clenched his hands together before him. "Yes, there's something I want to talk to you about."

Oh, no, here it comes. He's going to lower the boom. If he asks me directly, I'll have to say yes. I can't lie about the album any longer.

"Yes?" She swallowed hard, but the lump in her throat didn't move.

"Would you be my wife?"

Chapter Four

Music filtered through the air from a sidewalk café somewhere downriver. Violins sighed in accompaniment to April's intake of breath at Michael's shocking proposal.

His wife? Was he joking? She felt like she'd stepped into one of the soap operas she'd watched faithfully once upon a time with her mother. The dashing hero would pop the question to an unsuspecting heroine while sappy music set the mood for the romantic encounter.

April clung to her balloon as a cool breeze whisked across the water. A boat continued its languid journey along the river, carrying the men who lit the fires, delighting spectators along the way as each cauldron ignited with the touch of a mighty torch. The dark river came alive with crackling flames shooting sparks high into the night, and the soothing scent of burning wood lulled April into thinking she'd heard Michael wrong.

"Did you say *wife?*" Her voice pitched unusually high as she scrutinized his tense facial features.

"I know it sounds crazy. I've been trying to think of the best way to broach the subject. I thought the gifts and surprises would help ease the way."

"That's insane. You barely know me. Why would you want to marry me?"

A woman nearby turned her head, an inquisitive look on her face.

Michael pursed his lips tightly and scratched the back of his neck in contemplation. "That's not what I said."

April shifted away from the railing and lowered her voice.

"Wait a minute. First you ask me to marry you, then you say you didn't. Is this some kind of joke?"

"I asked you to be my wife. I didn't ask you to marry me." He seemed almost embarrassed to say it, especially with several bystanders now obviously tuned in to the conversation.

"Oh, and there's a difference?"

"Yes. Look, can we go back to my office where we can have more privacy and hopefully I can explain it a little better?"

"No."

"April, I really don't want to discuss the details here in public."

"I mean, no, I won't marry you. Or be your wife, or anything else along those lines."

The woman near her opened her mouth in shock.

"Don't say no until you hear me out."

"No. That's final. When I get married, it'll be for love and no other reason."

She stepped off the bridge and quickly walked away from the river, from the man who'd occupied too many unbidden thoughts since he'd shown up in her office yesterday.

Michael hurried to catch up. "Then why did you do it for fun?"

She stopped so fast, he took two more steps forward before he realized she'd halted. "What did you say?"

Looking back, he searched her face, his own a strained map of uncertainty. "If you'll come back to my office, I'll explain."

"I don't see why you can't explain right here, right now. I'm running out of patience, and I'm tired and hungry."

"There's something in my office I need to show you, and I promise I'll buy you dinner—if you'll let me."

She studied him, looking for the crack, the false representation that would confirm her suspicions he was up to no good. But she found none. Strangely, he almost appeared worried, unlike the self-assured business genius who'd breezed into her office yesterday. Her natural instinct told her not to give in, but something deeper urged her to give him a chance.

April lowered her crossed arms, and the balloon bopped her upside the head. She stared into his dark eyes. "Once we get back there, you've got five minutes to explain, then I'm out of there. And forget the dinner. I'm too tired to be sociable."

Michael walked quietly beside the outspoken, determined spit-fire, amazed at her unwillingness to yield. He'd never thought he'd like that in a woman, but, surprisingly, he found he did. A lot of things about this particular woman appealed to him, which made his proposal all the more enticing.

To him.

Now all he had to do was convince her, and he had five minutes to do it. No problem. He'd solved business fluctuations and failures in less time than that. He was the golden boy who never failed.

With a stiff gait, April walked into his office as he held the door, leaving it open, since everyone had gone home for the day. He stepped to the back of his desk, stationing himself in front of the large window overlooking the breathtaking Providence skyline sparkling in the darkening night. All for her benefit: a glimpse of his success. He needed every advantage in his court to sway her opinion of him.

"The clock is ticking," she pointed out as she slung herself into one of the chairs before his desk.

"Right." He cleared his throat. "I recently came across something that made no sense at all to me, so I set out to find its source and destroy it. Along the way, I became sidetracked by details and decided to see where the ride would go. Just for fun. But then a situation here in the office prompted me to change course and alter the destination."

"What on earth are you talking about?" With an elbow propped on the arm of the chair, she leaned the side of her head into her hand. "Why would anything in *your* office have anything to do with me?"

"I need a wife, and you're the perfect choice."

Instead of being flattered, she frowned. "I'm perfect? Me, the klutz, the workaholic, the queen of uncoordinated dressing? Yeah, right. If I'm perfect, what does that make you?"

"The holder of the trump card."

Again she frowned, this time shaking her head. "Look, by my watch, you have two minutes left. You haven't convinced me of anything except that you have a few screws loose."

Michael stood behind his desk, both hands braced, then gently pushed the big manila envelope forward. "Then see if this will convince you."

April's eyes grew wide as she watched the envelope come toward her. Real fear flashed in her clear blue eyes, and she drew back as though danger lurked inside that envelope. Michael felt a mixture of relief, knowing he had the upper hand, and remorse for putting her through this.

"What is it?" she asked in a shaky voice.

"I have a feeling you already know. It's the something I came across that made no sense to me. Open it, April, and tell me if it makes any sense to you. Maybe you can help me understand."

Michael finally sat down. He'd gained the upper hand and could now negotiate with confidence.

She reached for the envelope with the hand that still clutched the balloon. Looking up, she seemed annoyed and jerked the string free. The balloon floated to the ceiling, and the string gently rocked in the imperceptible current of circulated air.

Pulling the envelope to the edge of the desk, she hesitantly unwound the string clasp and slipped her hand inside. Before the album was even halfway out, she choked on a gasp and quickly released the evidence.

She sat back with heavy resignation. "I can explain."

"I thought you might be able to."

She licked her dry lips and rubbed her forehead. Her eyes appeared cloudy and sad, but she never looked directly at Michael.

"Can I have some water?"

Without a word, Michael went out of the office, quickly drew a cupful from the water cooler, and returned with her request.

"Thanks." She swallowed with heavy gulps until she'd drained all the water. Then she crushed the paper cup while her gaze remained fixed on the envelope on his desk. "I'll understand if you hate me, but really, it was nothing personal against you. It was all a joke. An April Fool's joke."

"But I didn't even know you. Why would you play a joke on me?"

"It wasn't on you. It was on my friends. Oh, God." She clenched and unclenched her hands on the arms of the chair. "You see, my friends and I have had this tradition of playing April Fool's jokes on one another, and the best one wins. We have a girl's night out, and the winner doesn't have to pay for dinner."

"Now I'll ask one of *your* questions. What does that have to do with me?" Michael kept his voice calm, not wanting to frighten her into leaving.

"Of the four of us, I'm the last one who's single. Well, Christine's not married yet, but she just got engaged. They're always teasing me about working too hard and never finding the right man. One day, feeling particularly vulnerable and sorry for myself, I was browsing through some files on my computer and came across the photos Tim took at the Gellar wedding."

Aha, Michael thought, *the pieces are coming together.* He sat back, his hands tented in front of his mouth to hide his amusement.

"Before I knew it, I was editing the photos for fun just to see what I'd look like as a bride. I thought . . ." She cleared her throat. "Well, when I saw you in several of the photos, I thought you would make a handsome groom."

"So, you produced this album to show your friends you'd gotten married? Why would they believe it? I mean, wouldn't they have been invited to your wedding?"

"I had gone on vacation just before that, visiting a cousin in Florida, and I told them it was all a spur-of-the-moment thing while away. Naturally they only believed me for about two minutes. They know me better than that. But we had a great laugh about my phony wedding, and I won the prize for the night."

"And the notation, 'April's Fool'?"

"Oh. You saw that." She shook her head. "I don't know. It was just a last-minute twist on the name. Guess I was the fool for doing it."

He nodded in agreement, but, sitting there across from him, looking vulnerable and sheepish, she was rather appealing. But then, she'd been appealing when she boldly blasted him out too.

"What I don't get is how you got the album," she murmured.

"The restaurant sent it over. I guess one of the waitresses recognized me and knew where I worked."

"Really?" she asked in a slightly testy tone.

"You shouldn't have left it there if you didn't want anyone to know your little secret."

"It wasn't on purpose. Like I said, we had a great time that night celebrating Christine's engagement and my winning joke. I lost track of the album, thought it was in my car, and didn't think about it again until a few days later. By the time I checked back with the restaurant, they had no idea what'd happened to it."

Silence prevailed as Michael studied April and she studied him. He believed her. The story was too crazy not to believe.

"I'm sorry, Michael. It had nothing to do with you. It was a stupid, foolish thing to do, but no one got hurt."

Michael rose and glanced leisurely out the window. He could see her reflection in the glass, the fear on her face. Even though he wasn't out to frighten her, he could certainly use it to his advantage.

Turning abruptly, he paced slowly around the desk until he reached the corner closest to April's chair. Settling one hip on the wood desktop, he leaned toward her.

"Do you know what something like this could do to my career? Do you know how important everything I do, say, or imply is to the person I report to? If it were discovered that I was not completely honest with them, who knows where my next paycheck might come from?"

"Are you saying you couldn't be married and work here?" Her face tightened with confusion.

"No, I'm saying they like to know everything about their personnel, especially key executives. And if a secret is kept and they find out later—well, there's just no telling what kind of retaliation might come my way. I might not even get the promotion that I'm up for."

April's mouth opened wide. "Oh, no, Michael! That's awful. I mean—wait. If no one knows about it but us, how could this all come crashing down around you?"

He chuckled. "Well, it wouldn't, or shouldn't, except that I'm not the only one who's seen the pictures."

She gasped. "Your boss?"

"No, but the boss' nephew and the receptionist have. I threw them off the trail, but you know how these things fester. One casual remark to the wrong person and—*bam!*—my career is as unco-ordinated as my two left feet."

"I see. Well"—she rose and reached for the envelope—"you can be sure I won't tell a soul. I'll just take this album home and hide it at the back of my closet."

He slapped his hand down on the album, halting her attempt to pull it forward. "I have a better idea." He pulled the envelope away, out of her reach. A startled expression met his let's-make-a-deal stare.

"But you just said . . . Wait a minute." She straightened and braced one hand on her hip. "Are you trying to scam me? If I didn't know better, I'd think you were about to hit me up for money. Blackmail."

Michael laughed softly and shook his head.

"No, you're not, are you? But you *do* have a plan, right? A devious one."

"April, I'm shocked that you would think of me as devious. And you, the very pillar of goodness—"

"All right, cut the malarkey. So I'm no angel. Big deal. Name someone who is. Regardless of what you think, I have strong values and convictions."

"Good, then this should be easy."

"This?"

"I want you to be my wife."

"I already told you I'd never marry anyone except for love."

"And I told you I didn't ask you to marry me. I just want you to be my wife. Look." He opened the album to the first page. "Don't we make a great couple? We both look so happy, like it was inevitable."

"That's not funny."

"It wasn't meant to be. I take my job seriously, and so does my boss. You see, if he were to see these pictures and think I'm hiding something, he'd lose respect for me. But if I tell him I got married on the QT and we're trying to get our bearings, he'd be thrilled. The old man has this hang-up about key workers. He thinks that the ones who are married are more stable. I'm the logical choice for this promotion, but I'm single. April, if you will agree to be my wife—temporarily, of course—I think I can pull it off without even trying."

April shook her head from side to side. With her mouth agape, a tiny gasp escaped. "You're nuts. We're in the twenty-first century, and you think that having a wife will win you a job? That is complete nonsense."

"No different from what made you doctor up some wedding photos to show off in front of your friends. How desperate do you have to be to do that?"

A deafening silence surrounded them like a lynch mob. April's lips tightened. Her fists clenched. But when fire burned behind her clear blue eyes, Michael knew he'd gone too far.

"Oooph," she growled, then turned and headed toward the door.

"Wait, April! I didn't mean that like it sounded."

She stood in the doorway, her back to him. "I am *not* desperate to be married. But if I were, you can be sure you'd be the last person to park his shoes under *my* bed."

She then continued out the door, down the hallway, and into the lobby without even a glance back. *No!* His hard-nosed business tactics hadn't worked. She hadn't fallen for the guilt trip or even the hard-luck story, and his sharp jab had only managed to anger her. What was left? How could he get her to see how important this was?

Pacing in front of the window again, he struggled with how to make her see the light. Experience had taught him that the opponent must realize the consequences of his or her action before he or she could come around to a reasonable decision.

His decision.

Perhaps a little scare might be in order.

April ran out of the elevator as though she were escaping pure evil. She quickly ran into her office to gather her things and get out of the building.

"What'd you do with the balloons?" Tim asked as he shut down his computer and prepared to leave too.

"Gave them away."

"Geez, April. Isn't that a bit harsh?"

She whipped around to face him. "Harsh? Do you want to know what *harsh* is? *Harsh* is someone taking your words and twisting them around until they choke you. *Harsh* is taking advantage of a situation no matter how many people get hurt. *Harsh* is using someone's emotions against them to get what you want."

Tim backed up and put on his jacket. "Oh. I assume there's more to your story than just giving away the balloons, but this obviously isn't a good time."

"Exactamundo."

She waved a silent good-bye to Tim and left as fast as her feet could carry her. The parking garage, a block away, had never seemed farther. Her clogs echoed in the half-empty cinder-block structure as she rushed to her beat-up old car, then fumbled with the lock.

Once inside, she leaned heavily into the headrest, closing her eyes with the hope of erasing the nightmare she'd awoken to.

Michael Goode had schemed his way onto her good side, then broadsided her with his outrageous suggestion. Imagine, pretending to have a wife just to get a promotion. How archaic! Not to mention his blatant insinuation that she was so desperate for a husband, she'd had to make one up. *The nerve.*

She started her car and waited for the old engine to smooth out its fits and coughs. She might not have a lot, but she had her dignity, and she intended to keep it. If he needed a wife, let him find someone else.

By the time she got home, her pulse had slowed to a mere trot, and her anger toward Michael had lessened just enough to let hunger take over.

She distracted her brain by heating up some leftover meat loaf and a baked potato. Midway through her halfhearted meal, the phone rang.

"April, did you forget our shopping trip?"

The meat loaf sank lower in her stomach. "Mom, I'm sorry. Yes, I got tied up at work and completely forgot our plans for the mall. I should have called."

"Are you okay? You sound tired."

"I am. It was an exhausting day."

Her mother sighed that hopeless, motherly sigh. "Honey, you work much too hard." *Here it comes.* "You need to get out more, be with friends, meet new people." By *new,* she meant *male.*

"I have plenty of friends, Mom, but I also have a career, which I love. Today just happened to be one of those days." Far from an ordinary day at the office, since Michael Goode had come along.

"When was the last time you went on a date? You must meet some men in your line of work, don't you?"

True to character, her mother thought that a job was just another playing field in which to search for a husband. The irony of that thought smacked truer than she'd realized. She'd *found* a "husband" right there at work, and because of it she now had more headaches.

But her mother wouldn't be satisfied until she had an answer, something to latch on to and give her hope for a hopeless daughter.

"As a matter of fact, Mom, I did meet someone at work. It's nothing serious, though. We're just friends."

Ha! A *friend* was the last thing Michael Goode would call her right now. He'd very nearly wanted to strangle her for the stunt she'd pulled. But with true business-viper tactics, he'd turned it around to his favor. Her mistake was now his, as he called it, trump card. If she didn't play along, who knew what he'd do?

"Really? Have you been out? When can I meet him?"

Typical Mom questions. Questions she didn't want to answer, or couldn't.

"Yes, we went to WaterFire tonight, but we haven't had a real date. It's more of a business relationship right now."

Her mother crooned. "WaterFire! That's so romantic. What a great way to start a relationship."

If she only knew. "Don't get your hopes up, Mom. It probably won't go anywhere. He's very busy with his own career."

As soon as she said it, she knew what her mother was thinking.

"How busy? Is he so tied to his job that he won't pay attention to you? I don't want to see you get hurt again. He's not another Stan, is he?"

Yes, he is. Only worse. "Mom, give me some credit. I know enough not to make that mistake again." Did she really?

"Good. Not that Stan was bad. I liked him. He just didn't spend enough time with you. Once he gets settled in his career, maybe he'll come back for you as he promised. Have you heard from him lately?"

"Mom, you have to accept that Stan is ancient history. I have. I don't even give him a second thought anymore."

Except every day when she squashed a creepy insect or flushed the toilet. And every day since she'd met Michael Goode, who had the capacity to outdo Stan's ruthless climb to the top. Imagine, thinking that a marriage would get him a promotion. Sadly, her mother would probably agree with him.

"I promise to make it up to you, Mom. We'll go shopping another night."

"Okay. We'll see you on Sunday, right?"

"Yes, I'll be there for dinner."

"Did you want to invite your new friend?"

"No!" She bit back the curse on her tongue for snapping at her mother. "I don't . . . we don't know each other well enough yet. It's all very new."

"I understand. We wouldn't want to scare him off by meeting the parents so soon." Her mother giggled as though the real scheme would be on their part.

"Right. Okay. I'll see you Sunday, and again, I'm sorry for standing you up tonight."

April looked at her half-eaten dinner and wondered why she'd led her mother to believe such an untruth. Her relationship with Michael wasn't new; it was nonexistent. In a moment of weakness, she'd created a pretend wedding, but, like a movie, it wasn't real. And no matter how much Michael pleaded with her, she wasn't going any further with the sham.

Chapter Five

The next morning April quietly entered the building, carefully checking around each corner to be sure Michael didn't ambush her. She rode the elevator alone, then peeked out in both directions before she got off. At the door to Web Works, she peered inside before entering.

No sign of Michael Goode anywhere.

Relieved, she eased into her daily routine, anxious to forget last night, the day before, and, most of all, that dumb wedding album. What had she been thinking?

Tim looked up from his screen, glancing over his glasses at her until she settled down and turned on her computer. April purposely avoided eye contact, knowing she couldn't hide her emotional turmoil from him.

"Michael Goode called," he announced. "He said you can pick up what you left in his office anytime."

April nodded stiffly. "Thanks." *Good, he'd come to his senses and forgotten the whole stupid wife idea.*

"His office, huh?" Tim continued. "Was that before or after you flew in and out of here? At that time of night most of the building is empty except for us diehards, so it must've been very quiet and lonely way up there on the fifteenth floor." April focused on her screen, watching the boot-up process with great interest. "What did you leave up there? An earring? Your handbag? Dignity?"

"Knock it off, Tim. Nothing happened. We just went to his office to . . . talk. I was only there a few minutes."

Tim snickered. "A lot can happen in a few minutes."

51

She shot a fierce warning at him. "I said knock it off. There's nothing between us."

With a comical snort, Tim turned back to his computer. "Right. Nothing. Guess I'd better go get my eyes checked. This prescription is making me see things that don't exist."

April threw a pen at him, and he just laughed, which only added to her aggravation. But it didn't all stem from Tim's inferences. She was angry that Michael had tried to manipulate her, angry that he didn't see the humor in the innocent prank, but mostly angry that she'd done such a foolish thing as make that album in the first place. It had been an impulsive act born out of frustration. She'd only wanted to see what it would be like to be a bride. And her friends had loved it!

Was Michael right? Was she so desperate for a husband that she had to make one up in order for her friends to accept her?

No, he wasn't right. She was happy with her life, happy with her job. She didn't need a husband to factor into the equation, regardless of what her mother thought.

She didn't.

With a sudden urge to put this all to rest, she shoved back her chair and started for the door. "I'll be right back," she sneered over her shoulder as she charged ahead. Her destination, Gellar Investments.

But when she arrived, Shelley, the receptionist, told her that Mr. Goode was in a meeting.

"That's okay. I just came to get something I left yesterday. If I could just step into his office for one sec—"

Shelley peered quizzically at her. "In his office? I don't recall you being here yesterday. What was your name again?"

A little warning went off in April's head. Of course she didn't recall April's being there. She'd already left for the day—everyone had. "April Vaillancourt." No need to say she'd been there last night.

"Hmm. I don't remember the name, but you do look familiar." Shelley excused herself to answer a call but continued to study April. The call completed, she then rose. "Why don't you tell me what you left, and I'll just run in and get it."

"Oh, no, that's really not necessary. I know you're very busy. I promise, I'll pop in and out—"

"It's no problem. The phones are quiet this early in the morning." She walked across the lobby and put her hand on the doorknob to Michael's office. "Now, what am I looking for?"

April saw the hopelessness of getting around guard dog Shelley. Whether she was superefficient or just plain nosy, Shelley had the advantage and wasn't letting go.

"It's, ah, it's a book. Well, actually, it's probably in a manila envelope. A big one. Very heavy. It should be right on his desk."

"A book, in a manila envelope." Shelley stepped into the office and returned a minute later. "I don't see anything on his desk, and there's no manila envelope anywhere in plain sight. There was one curious thing, though—" The phone interrupted, and Shelley smiled apologetically as she went to answer.

April wrung her hands. She'd hoped she could retrieve the album without having to face Michael. Maybe she could convince Shelley to have it sent down to her later.

Finished with the call, Shelley said, "If it's really important, I could ring Mr. Goode in the conference room."

"Oh, no, don't bother. But when he gets out, if you could ask him for the album and have it sent—"

"Album?" April watched Shelley's face turn from confusion to interest to enlightenment. "The album! That's why you look familiar." She lowered her voice, even though all the other office doors were closed. "*You're* the bride! So, it's true? He really did get married? Oh my God, I can't believe it. He denied it to the hilt, but I told Kenny—"

"Kenny? Other people know?"

"Well, just me and Kenny as far as I know. Oh, congratulations!" She clasped April's hands in hers, her long red nails digging in. "You really took us by surprise, I mean, so sudden, and . . . oh!" Once again, Shelley's face transformed as another realization took hold. "Well, I guess that explains the other thing in his office."

"Other thing?"

Shelley smiled and winked, but before she could say another

word, a door opened down the corridor and a parade of suits exited. The last one was the tallest, the sharpest, and certainly the most handsome. April couldn't help but sigh as Michael Goode walked toward her while the other men split off into their offices.

"Good morning. I see you got my message." His tone was polite but edged with uncertainty.

"Yes, thanks. I just came to get it."

With a reserved half smile, Michael motioned toward his office. "Come in."

Once inside, April quickly scanned the desk. Shelley was right. No envelope. "Where is it?"

"Right there." He pointed behind the door.

When April turned, she saw the white balloon with the teddy bear inside bumping against the ceiling, the string lazily flowing with the air current.

"The balloon? I meant the album. Where's the album?"

He sat down, leaning back to stretch his legs. "Oh, that's safely tucked away."

"But I thought you said I could come get it."

"I said you could come get what you left here. You left your balloon. The album was *delivered to me.*"

"But—" April stepped back to the door and closed it quietly. "*She* thinks we're married! Why did you show her?"

"I didn't. *She* was the one who received the delivery—with no name on it, I might add."

"But she said someone else saw it too. Kenny?"

"Yes, Kenny Gellar. Mr. Gellar's nephew. I told you all that last night."

April put her hands to her head. "Oh, God. You have to tell them. You can't let them believe it."

"Why not? Like I said, it can only help my career. In this company, marriage means stability, and stability means endurance. Gellar wants a CEO who is here for the long haul. I'm that man, regardless of whether or not I'm married. But if it'll make the old man happy, I'll be anything he wants."

Michael propped his hands behind his head and grinned like a sated cat. April's blood boiled at the thought of his manipulative ladder-climbing. Was that a male thing? Had Stan lied and cheated his way to the top too? Maybe she couldn't stop Michael, but she certainly wasn't going to help.

"Well, not at my expense." With her hand on the knob, she fired back, "You'd better find yourself another wife," then opened the door.

Before she could get her bearings as to which way was out, she heard Michael behind her.

"Oh, sweetheart, you forgot something."

She turned to face him, his outstretched hand holding the balloon, while behind her Shelley sighed. He'd calculated this move for the benefit of the receptionist.

Michael eased his arm across her shoulders while turning her toward the lobby door. "Come on, honey, I'll walk you to the elevator." He ushered her out the door before she could protest a word in front of Shelley.

"I suppose you're very proud of yourself for that flagrantly deceptive display!" April faced the elevator doors so she didn't have to see his mocking eyes. When he didn't answer, she glanced sideways and saw that he studied her with genuine interest.

"I admit it."

"I don't want her, or anyone, thinking that we're married."

He reached for her left hand, pulling it toward him, and gently wrapped the balloon string around her ring finger. He slowly stroked the knuckle with his thumb while searching her eyes.

"And I don't want this to get ugly, because I really do like you. But I have a call in to my attorney to see what my options are."

"An attorney? For what?"

"Any number of things. Defamation of character, unlawful use of my photograph without my permission, damage to my career. I'm sure he can round up a half dozen claims. That doesn't mean any of them would stick, but we could tie you up in court for years."

"You wouldn't!"

"I'm a desperate man, April. I need this small favor from you, and I think you owe me. It won't cost you anything except a few dinners, cocktail parties—you know, things married couples do in public. I'll foot all the expenses—your clothes, hair, nails, anything you want. You might actually enjoy it. Come on, what do you say?"

She pushed the Down button, and when the door opened, she stepped inside, tugging at the balloon to follow.

"Try a temp service."

On his way back to his office, Michael caught Shelley smiling behind the pen pressed against her lips.

"That was so sweet. Michael, I never would have guessed you to be the romantic type, and so considerate."

"No? Why?"

She shrugged. "You're usually so . . . so . . ."

"So what?"

"Full of yourself. Sorry. I don't mean it in a bad way. It's just the way you present yourself—confident, all-knowing, determined. Don't get me wrong, they're fine qualities, just not the kind that'll get you a good woman."

"Really? I can see that I've missed the boat by not consulting with you all these years."

Again, Shelley shrugged and waved a noncommittal hand. "Nah, you've done fine. But this time you did real good. I like her. She seems very genuine. A bit nervous, but I guess that's to be expected under the circumstances." Shelley winked.

"Yes, marriage is new to both of us."

"That too, but I mean, you know . . ." Shelley patted her stomach.

Pregnant? Did she think April was pregnant? Why?

And then it hit him. The suddenness of the marriage, the secrecy, the teddy bear balloon. Shelley thought it all added up to a shotgun wedding.

Perfect!

"Shelley, I have some calls to make. Would you see that no one disturbs me until I say so? Unless, of course, it's Mrs. Goode."

Beaming a smile at her superior, Shelley assumed her professional face as a visitor entered the lobby. Michael retreated to his office and leaned against the door until it clicked shut.

Married *and* expecting. What could be sweeter? He smiled to himself as his plan took on a life of its own. He'd have that promotion in no time at all, and maybe a little fun tossed in for good measure.

Going to his desk, he picked up the phone and called his attorney friend. "Dan, what kind of lawsuit could I bring on someone who'd used my picture without my permission and in a way that could damage my reputation?"

"What?" .

Michael chuckled. "Let me explain." He filled Dan in on everything, including his plan. "But I'm having trouble convincing her to play along, so I thought if I hung a lawsuit over her head, she'd change her mind. Not that I'd do it."

"Michael, what you're doing is as bad as what she did, if not worse. It's blackmail, not to mention misrepresentation to Gellar. What about a year from now, or longer? Will you keep up the pretense of a marriage indefinitely?"

"Simple. I'll say the impulsive marriage didn't work, and we got divorced. People get divorced every day."

A grumbling sound came through the phone. Michael frowned. Lawyers wanted everything in nice, tidy packages.

"I want you to know, I don't approve of any of this, Michael. Marriage is not something to be taken lightly, even if it does advance your career. Legally, yes, you could slap a halfhearted lawsuit on her for any of the things you mentioned. Realistically, I doubt you'd get a judge to see your point. No damage was done, no monetary gain, and your reputation certainly wasn't compromised in any way."

"But she wouldn't know that unless she got her own lawyer, and I just don't see her doing that."

Another grumbling sound. "You are a financial genius, Michael, and I value all the help you've given me over the years, but when it comes to women and relationships, you stink. Take some friendly advice. Never underestimate a woman."

"Don't ask!" April unwound the balloon string from her finger and let the bear sail off into a corner after Tim quizzed her with a tilted head and raised eyebrows.

"Trouble in paradise?"

"It's far from paradise. The man is positively . . . self-centered!"

"Yeah, I can see that. He gives you balloons, candy, flowers."

"Drop it, okay? There's a lot more to it, and I don't care to discuss it."

"Then would you care to discuss Stan?"

She glared at him for a moment, confused by the shift in gears. "Stan who?"

"Stan Tragar. Your former boyfriend."

"Why would I want to talk about him?"

"Because he called while you were schmoozing upstairs. He says he'll be by at lunchtime."

"*What?* Are you messing with me, Tim? 'Cause I'm really not in the mood." Tim solemnly shook his head. "What did he say? Why is he coming here?"

Tim held up a hand. "I said nothing. I asked nothing. I merely told him you were out of the office at the moment, and he said to tell you he'd be here at lunchtime."

She plunked down in her seat, the weight of the news too heavy to bear. What did Stan want? She hadn't seen him in almost four years. As if dealing with Michael Goode for the last few days hadn't been enough, now Stan. What more could a single woman take?

"What are you going to do?" Tim finally asked after April had time to collect herself.

"Nothing. Stan means nothing to me anymore."

Not entirely the truth, because she knew that once she looked into those gray eyes, she'd remember the feelings she once had for him. She could only hope she'd also remember the pain he'd caused her.

"Just whistle if you need help."

April nodded appreciatively at Tim. He didn't want to see her hurt either. Their official relationship might be boss/employee, but its roots stemmed from the strong friendship they'd forged years ago as co-workers.

The morning ticked by with little else said as they both clicked away at their computers. Tim left for an early lunch, promising to bring back a sandwich so she could use that as an excuse not to go out with Stan.

April immediately picked up the phone and called a friend.

"Christine, I'm in big trouble. Stan's back in town, and he's headed over here."

"April, why did you allow that?"

"I didn't. He left a message with Tim saying he'd be by. What do I do?"

"No matter what, you cannot leave there with him. You know if he gets you alone, he'll have you all tied up in knots. You've never been able to fight his persuasiveness."

"I know, but I don't want to air our past right in front of Tim either. This is a place of business."

"If I weren't over an hour away, I'd come there myself and run interference. Just tell him you're busy and send him packing. Go out into the lobby if you have to. Just *do not* give in to him."

When she didn't answer, Christine yelled into the phone, "April!"

"Yes, sorry. I'm just a little distracted."

"You always were with Stan around."

"No, it's not just him, it's . . ." She couldn't stop thinking about Michael and the confusion of the wedding album.

"What? Is something else going on? April, you know you can't keep secrets from me, so you might as well spill it now."

Of course. The reason she'd called Christine in the first place was to get her sound advice. The two of them had been like sisters since high school. Each one took care of the other. Christine had a fiancé now and didn't need taking care of, but April still did.

After a brief rundown on the whole Michael Goode episode, April sighed. "So what should I do?"

"Why are you asking for advice? I thought you gave him your answer."

"Well, I did, but now he's threatening a lawsuit—"

"Then go along with the marriage thing."

"But I'd feel like such a fraud, pretending to be married to someone I don't even know."

"That didn't seem to bother you when you created the album."

April gritted her teeth at her friend's lethal observation. "Don't remind me. He's already made that perfectly clear."

Christine let out a little chuckle. "You know what I think? I think there's more to his offer than you're saying, or at least more than you'll admit to."

"What are you talking about? There isn't anything more. He wants me to pretend to be his wife so he can get a promotion."

"Exactly. Sounds like you're dragging up feelings from the 'Stan' years."

"Well, yeah. Stan did have only one thing on his mind—climbing to the top. Michael is the same."

"Your soap opera background is showing. Just because one man did something to you doesn't mean the next one will. Besides, if you're not involved with Michael, how would you get hurt?"

April hesitated, unsure how to respond.

"Or are you involved? There's more, isn't there? Tell me, April, why does this man have you so tongue-tied?"

Reluctantly April explained about the flowers, candy, and balloons. She laughed about how much fun they'd had handing out free balloons to kids.

"And? Come on, there's more to it than that, or you wouldn't be dragging your feet."

April heaved a resigned sigh. "We kissed."

"Well, then, I'd say we're talking a whole new ball game here. As your friend—one who has seen her share of losers, I might add—I want you to know that a man doesn't go through that many hoops just to get someone to do him a favor. If that's all he wanted, he would've offered you a lump sum or paid someone else. No, he wants *you* to play the role. Why? He's interested."

"But only until he gets his promotion. After that, I'm day-old bread."

"You don't know that, but even if it's so, you're going in with your eyes open this time. Play along, enjoy the parties and pampering, and have a good time."

"I was afraid you'd say that. My head keeps telling me the same thing. I mean, after all, I did make a fool of the guy. But my heart says no, it's not right. Marriage should not be pretended."

"Again, that didn't seem to bother you when you made that wedding album."

April grunted. "Somehow I knew coming to you would give me the reality check I needed."

"Or the shove in the right direction."

They both laughed.

"One more thing, April. This would also be the perfect white lie to get Stan out of your life. Tell him you have a new husband, and watch him slither away."

"I couldn't do that. It's a blatant lie."

"You've put up with enough of *his* lies over the years. This half-truth is only a drop in the ocean."

April thanked her friend for listening and promised to let her know what happened. Now she just needed the courage to follow through with the second dumbest thing she'd ever done.

Chapter Six

Gellar Investments. How may I direct your call?"

"Michael Goode, please." April's voice quavered in direct opposition to Shelley's clear, crisp greeting.

"I'm sorry, but Mr. Goode is on a conference call. May I take a message?"

"Yes, would you ask him to get back to April Vaillancourt at his earliest convenience?"

Immediately, Shelley's tone changed. "Oh, Mrs. Goode! I can interrupt if you'd like—"

"No, no, please don't. Just have him call when he's free."

Mrs. Goode? April put the phone down and held her hands to her head. What was she doing? This was even crazier than the wedding album. What if she couldn't pull it off? If instead she ruined the promotion for Michael?

She raised her head and focused on the balloon now losing its altitude, remembering his tender touch when he'd wrapped the string around her finger. A tightness in her chest warned her there could be more at stake here than ruining Michael's career. He'd awakened a hardened heart with his smile, his attentiveness. The night they'd given away the balloons, she'd seen his delight at making the kids happy. What if she expected more of him than she got? What if she gave more than necessary? Could she stand the loss when it was over?

The phone rang and startled her from the dreaded thoughts.

"Web Works."

"We must be on the same wavelength, because I was just about to call when Shelley handed me your message."

Warmth oozed through April's veins at the sound of Michael's soothing voice. "Oh? About what?"

"I thought we could meet for lunch downstairs and talk."

"I can't. I . . . have plans."

She didn't see any reason to explain the Stan thing. Besides, once Stan got there, she'd get rid of him just as fast, and she sure didn't want to deal with both of them at the same time.

"I'm staying here for lunch, since I'm in the middle of tying up this project. But I did want to speak with you. If I'm done in about two, three hours, could you see me then?"

He lowered his voice. "I just cleared my calendar."

The warmth spread to her face, and she was glad he couldn't see her silly grin.

No sooner had Tim returned and set a sandwich near her keyboard than she looked up and saw the face of the man who'd stripped her of her self-esteem when she was too young to know what had happened. He'd stolen her love too, young love, the kind that fairy tales are built on and futures are made from. She'd cursed at that face in her dreams and vowed never to let him or any other man take her self-respect again.

But one look at Stan's eager grin and smiling gray eyes, and April felt herself helplessly drawn into his familiar, charismatic pull. She told herself to look away, but she couldn't. It had been so long since she'd seen him, and he looked wonderful. Refreshed, happy, and . . . successful.

The last reminder was enough to force her back to her game plan. Stan couldn't be trusted with her emotions. She must not give in to him, no matter what he said.

He opened his arms as he approached her desk. "April, you look fabulous."

She knew she didn't. She'd rushed out the door that morning with barely a thought to what clothes she'd thrown on. "Hello, Stan. What do you want?"

His hands still outstretched, he pleaded, "Maybe a little welcome hug would be nice, to start."

She shook her head. "You're four years too late."

He nodded, then lowered his voice. "I know this is awkward"—he glanced over at Tim—"so why don't we go downstairs and grab something to eat where we can talk more comfortably? I have a lot to catch you up on."

"Stan, I'm not comfortable talking to you anywhere. Now, if you don't mind, I have a lot of work to do."

He clasped his hands behind his back and rocked on his heels in front of her desk. "Forgive me for being such a fool all those years ago, but things have changed. I'm not the man I was then. I'd like to tell you what I've accomplished and how my life is headed in the right direction. Please, April, spare me a few minutes."

Maybe if she gave him a chance to say what was on his mind, she could then turn him away without guilt and be rid of him forever. She chanced a quick glance at Tim, who raised a mocking eyebrow.

"Tim, do you mind if I just step out into the foyer for a minute?"

Surprised that she'd involved him by asking his permission, he shrugged one shoulder. "Uh, sure. Make it quick."

She led the way out the door, and as soon as it closed, Stan caged her in his arms and kissed her unsuspecting lips. It took her a few seconds to recover from the shock of his overt display of affection. So unlike him. Certainly not something she'd experienced with him ever before.

Regardless, even this new tactic would not sway her from her goal to rid her life of him. With a shove against his expensive suit, she let him know she didn't appreciate the ambush.

"That better not happen again."

"April, honey, I missed you."

"Deaf ears, Stan, deaf ears."

"I know you have a right to hate me. I didn't exactly keep any of my promises, but I swear, I had every intention to. I just got sidetracked with the business aspect, and, well, quite honestly, you frightened me."

April faltered back as though she'd just been hit. Had she heard wrong? *"Frightened?* You were *frightened* of me? You've never been afraid of anything in your life, except missing out on another business opportunity."

He reached for her hand, but she tucked it behind her back. "I'm serious, April. You wanted so much, so fast. I didn't think I could deliver. I loved you, but the whole marriage thing really scared me. I'm older now, more mature, and I see that I've missed a great deal by not having you by my side."

A tiny spot in her heart opened up, the spot she'd buried, the spot that Stan had captured eight years ago. Could it be that he'd needed time to grow up? He'd chased a dream, only to find it lacking? Was the love she'd cast out for him finally coming back in return?

"Please, April, can we get some lunch and catch up on what we've missed—what I've missed?"

She heard Christine's voice: *Don't be alone with him. Don't let him deceive you again. You'll only get hurt in the end.*

But her heart ached with the hope that maybe she hadn't wasted all those years. He'd seen the error of his ways and had come back to claim the undying love he once professed. A few minutes of her time wouldn't hurt. God knows she needed some flattery to salve her bruised ego.

With a quick turn she looked inside the glass door to see Tim watching. She raised her hand to signal five minutes. Tim shook his head vehemently and waved for her to come back in.

No, she signaled again. She'd be back in five minutes. It was the least she could give Stan.

Tim grabbed for the phone as soon as they were out of his sight.

"Michael Goode, please."

"I'm sorry, but Mr. Goode is on the phone right now. May I take a message?"

"Shelley, it's Tim Houghton from Web Works."

"Oh, hi, Tim. How are you?"

He nearly melted at the friendly, sultry voice, but he didn't have time for chitchat. This was important. "I'm good, Shelley, but there's a problem with April, and I need to speak with Michael right away. It's urgent."

Shelley gasped, "Hold on."

Tim waited only a few seconds before the line opened again.

"Tim, what's wrong?"

"Mike, I don't know what to do. I'm not good in situations like this. . . . I think April needs to be rescued."

"Where is she? What happened?"

"She's down in the food court, I think. With Stan, her old boyfriend. Mike, the guy is bad news. He's totally wrong for her. She turns to putty around him, and I'm afraid he'll get her all tangled up in promises again. I tried to tell her not to go, but she didn't listen. I thought maybe you could go down and . . ."

"And do what? Why would she listen to me?"

"Well, I couldn't help but notice, you seem to have . . . an effect on her. I was hoping you could create a distraction, enough to snap her out of his spell."

"I see. Anything I should know about this guy? What am I up against?"

"Just that he's a slimeball, and April wasted eight years of her life pining for him."

"Got it."

Tim put down the phone and took a deep breath. April would have his head on a platter if she knew what he had done.

April watched the smooth lips forming words, words she'd longed to hear for years. Stan missed her, wanted her. He'd made executive vice president in charge of sales. He traveled all over the world, had an unlimited expense account, and had apartments both here and in London. But he had no one to share it all with. He'd love to have her by his side, on his arm at social events, and at his table when he entertained. . . .

Like the scratch of a stalled record, her brain came to a screeching halt at the true meaning of his words. She would be good for his career! Ah, yes, a familiar theme in her life lately. Only Stan's intentions were more subversive. He disguised it as wanting her, whereas Michael—

"There you are, sweetheart."

Behind her, Michael's voice jolted her from the fog she'd slipped into five minutes after seeing Stan. How had that happened? One minute she'd been ready to strangle Stan, the next, she'd melted under his gaze, waiting on his every word.

Before she could further analyze her weakness and hate herself for it, Michael leaned down and planted a fierce, hot kiss on her lips. Long enough to let her know she'd been kissed but too short for her even to close her eyes and enjoy it. That's when she looked across the table and saw for the first time an unsettled, tense Stan Tragar.

Without missing a beat, Michael continued. "I thought I was picking you up at your office, but Tim said you'd already come down here with an old friend." He turned to Stan, his hand outstretched. "Michael Goode."

Stan, practiced in cordiality, rose slightly and nodded with a forced smile. "Stan Tragar."

Michael pulled up a chair and slid it close to April, then looked from one to the other. Words hung in the air, just as the irony of Stan's last words—his proposition—hit her square in the face. They both wanted her to help further their careers. She didn't know what to say to either of them, and she certainly didn't want to say anything in front of *both* of them.

"You two are awfully quiet. Did I interrupt something?" Leave it to Michael to forge ahead. "You seemed to be engrossed in conversation when I walked up. . . . Wait." He held a finger in the air, as though suddenly enlightened. "You're *that* Stan. Ah, I get it. April's told me all about you. Sorry for barging in like that, but I get possessive around my bride. Can't get enough of her."

April had to stifle a laugh when she saw shock—real shock—on Stan's face. Michael noticed it too once he looked over.

"Oh, man, I thought you knew. April didn't tell you I'm her husband? Not surprising. It's all so new, sometimes it's hard for me to believe it's true. But we've got the pictures to prove it." He laughed and took her hand. "Now she just has to remember to put her ring on in the morning so the rest of the world knows it. Right, love?" He squeezed her left hand, assuring her he had it all under control.

Stan finally shook the shock from his face and nodded toward the happy couple. "Well, I guess congratulations are in order, then. I wish you both all the best."

"Thanks, Stan. That means a lot, coming from you." Michael's assurance almost had her convinced too.

April stood. "I'd better get back to the office. I promised Tim I'd only be gone five minutes. I never know what he'll do when I'm not there." She'd aimed that last statement at Michael, and he just grinned at her meaning.

He began to rise to accompany her, but Stan interrupted. "Michael, why not stay? I'd love to hear more about you, what business you're in."

April stiffened. The last thing she needed was these two talking business over her head, yet she feared that if she left, the talk might turn to her and the full-blown lie Michael had just perpetrated. Granted, it had been for her benefit, and she silently thanked him for that, but still, a lie is a lie. If she left, it might explode behind her back. If she stayed, she might detonate it herself.

She sat back down as Michael explained his position with Gellar Investments to a wide-eyed, impressed Stan, who countered that his growing assets might be in need of some good investment advice. April shuddered at the thought of these two powerful men working together in a business relationship. But then, that's what they were both best at: doing business, making deals.

Michael dug out a business card. "If you're interested, call my office for an appointment. I'm sure we can improve your situation." Then he stood and stepped aside for April to accompany him. "Let's get you back to work so you can finish your project, darling."

She noticed Stan's slight frown, as though it hadn't occurred to him that *her* job might be important too.

"Good-bye, Stan," she said with a tilt of her chin. "Thanks for thinking of me after all these years." The two men shook hands; then Michael escorted her out with a possessive hand at her back.

Once they reached the elevator, she turned to him. "I'm not entirely happy about what just happened, but I do thank you for rescuing me."

"I'm a sucker for a lady in distress." He smiled, then put a finger under her chin and searched her eyes. "I don't know what kind of power that guy has over you, but I'm glad I could help deflect it. He had to be a fool not to whisk you away when he had the chance. I'm glad he didn't."

She shook her head sadly. "Stan was everything I thought I wanted in a man, except for honest. If there's anything two people must have between them to make a relationship work, it's honesty."

"I thought it was love."

"Unless you're honest, you won't know that the love is true. It's easy to say *I love you,* much harder to say *I'd never lie to you.*"

He rubbed her chin with his thumb. "You're a wise woman."

She fought back a tear. "Wisdom born of pain."

They entered the elevator silently. April got off at her floor after Michael murmured, "I'll see you later," and continued up to his floor. After her little lecture about wisdom, she wondered if her planned meeting with him later was such a good idea.

As soon as she walked back into the office, Tim's gaze searched behind her to see if anyone followed.

"No, Tim, I'm alone. And, yes, Michael came to the rescue. I suppose I have you to thank for that."

He eyed her cautiously. "You aren't mad at me?"

"I was for about a minute, but then I realized you knew me better than I do. You knew I'd get sucked in by Stan's charisma again, didn't you?"

"Hey, I'm only looking out for myself here. If he swept you away, who would I have to rely on?"

She chuckled. "Thanks for the vote of confidence. One thing I *am* curious about though: why did you send Michael down there?"

Tim turned back to his screen and shrugged. "He's got bigger guns than me."

With that, the gaping friendship hole closed, and they both went back to work. It was almost four before April finished her project, shut down her system, and stood to stretch out the kinks.

"Tim, I'm calling it a day. I don't have the heart to start something new this late on a Friday afternoon. I'll come in early Monday morning."

"Okay. Have a good one."

April left and hesitated at the elevator, her finger poised over the Up button. It'd taken her longer to finish up her work because so much of her mind had been on Michael Goode. Even this elevator reminded her of him—his kiss that first day, his gentle touch with the balloon string. If she pushed that button, she'd open herself up to even more of him, and she didn't know if she could handle the disappointment in the end.

Taking a deep breath for fortification, she pushed, waited, then went up to meet her fate. As soon as she walked into Gellar's reception area, Shelley greeted her with a big smile.

"Mr. Goode said to go right in."

"Thank you."

"You look a little pale." Shelley lowered her voice to a whisper. "Would you like some crackers?"

Confused, April stuttered, "Uh, n-no, thanks anyway."

She headed down the hall to Michael's door, which stood ajar. Tapping lightly, she peered around the corner to see him at his desk behind a mountain of file folders.

"Sorry, I can come back another time if—"

He jumped up and went to greet her. "No! Come in, please." Brushing against her shoulder, he shut the door behind her and took the jacket she'd slung over her arm. "Here, have a seat."

He turned the two chairs in front of his desk to face each other, and, surprisingly, he sat in one. So, he wasn't going to play the shrewd businessman wielding power from behind the desk. She respected him for that; however, it made for a much more intimate meeting with him sitting just two feet in front of her.

Clever.

She took her seat and pretended casualness as she hung her purse over the arm of the chair. His manly scent floated around her, making her inhale too deeply. She coughed to disperse its alluring spell.

"So." Michael leaned forward, much too close. "What did you want to talk about?"

April squirmed, then sat straighter. "I thought a little more about your proposal—I mean, proposition, so to speak—and—"

"April, there's no appropriate word for what I asked of you, and I'm sorry. It was demeaning and cruel."

"Oh." She slumped back a bit, confused by her sudden sense of disappointment. If he'd changed his mind, then she was off the hook. She'd tormented herself all day for nothing and come up here on a futile mission.

On the other hand, could this be another tactic to win her over? Could he be playing against her guilt, telling her she didn't have to do it, knowing she would, especially after their encounter with Stan at lunch? Michael hadn't gotten to this level in business without learning a few tricks in human behavior.

"I suppose I deserved it," she continued. "And I did violate your rights."

"No real harm done."

She fiddled with her fingers, rubbing at a sharp cuticle. "So, you don't want to go through with this, then?"

He smiled. "I didn't say that. I thought you were the one opposed to it."

"I was, but this promotion sounded very important to you and—"

Michael slid forward and stilled her hands with his. "It is, April. It's what I've always wanted, what I've worked so hard for. Becoming CEO of this company would establish everything I've set out to do since I worked two jobs in high school. I'm thirty-six. If I go to another company, it could be years before this kind of opportunity comes my way again. I don't want to start over. I want to stay here. I like the people, I like the client base, and I've earned a respect for my aggressive business sense."

She pressed her lips together. Her eyes searched his. He looked so sincere, so nonthreatening. "I just don't know if I could be convincing enough."

"You won't have to convince anyone. Just be yourself, and let me do the convincing. It's my specialty."

His hands tightened around hers, and she knew that was exactly what he'd been doing from the moment he walked into her office to now—convincing her. With words, with touch, with emotion.

Boy, he was good.

"For how long?" April slipped her hands out from under Michael's.

He watched her shift uneasily. Apprehension tightened her features. But her eyes warmed as she gazed into his, the same eyes that had captured his interest when he'd stomped into her office. The same eyes that had glistened after their kiss in the elevator. They looked to him now for reassurance and promise.

For a moment, he'd almost forgotten why she was there, until he reminded himself they were in the middle of a business deal. He needed to get on with negotiating the details and not get bogged down in her sultry eyes and his growing desire.

"To say 'as long as it takes' would sound pretentious, but that's the only answer I have. Howard Gellar announced that his retirement will take effect on April 15, a little less than a year from now. However, he'll need to name his successor long before then to prepare the clients and make for a smooth transition. I'm guessing six months, maybe less, before he actually names me."

"Six months! How can we pretend we're married for six months?"

"It won't be six whole months of pretending. Just a few social events here and there to keep up appearances. And my offer still stands: if you need a dress, want your hair or nails done, whatever. It's all on me, or anything else for that matter. And when it's over, if you'll let me buy you something, it would be my pleasure."

"Payment for services rendered?" she quipped.

"Sort of like that, but don't make it sound so crude. You're doing me a big favor, and you deserve part of the reward."

She brushed her hand across her forehead. Wisps of curls waved at him, laughing at his attempt to sound sincere. Truth was, he was sincere. He would've given her anything she desired at that moment, and the depth of that emotion almost scared him. Michael Goode didn't scare easily.

He reached for her free hand, grasping the fingertips in what he hoped was a nonthreatening plea. "So, is that a yes?"

She chewed the inside of her cheek, then blinked her bright blue eyes at him. "I need tires."

Michael blinked back. "What?"

"Tires. My reward. My car is due for inspection in a few months, and the tires will never pass. I need four new tires."

He sat back and laughed heartily. "You are something, you know that? Another woman might've said a necklace, a ring, a trip. You want tires!" He straightened his tie and rose from the chair. "You got your tires, lady, and we've got a deal. Now, sit tight for a minute. There's someone I want you to meet."

Michael called Kenny's office and asked him to come in. Moments later, he arrived. "April, this is Kenny Gellar, my associate. Kenny, I'd like you to meet my wife, April."

As expected, Kenny was taken aback, but only for a second. "Really? I thought you said—"

"That it wasn't true? It's not. But after our conversation yesterday about the promotion, I decided to talk to April and see if we could come to some kind of agreement. She sympathized with my predicament and graciously agreed to pose as my wife when necessary."

His mouth slightly agape, Kenny looked from one to the other. "You're kidding, right? I mean, no one poses as husband and wife."

"No, I'm quite serious. Isn't that right, April?"

April merely bobbed her head once, then looked down.

"Here's the deal," Michael explained. "Whenever there are social functions or business events involving significant others, April will accompany me as my wife. We'll explain the secret wedding as a spontaneous decision made when we were away on vacation. You've seen the photos, so you can vouch for the legitimacy of the event and confirm it with your uncle. We'll need to be convincing for the old man, but I don't want to go overboard."

"Wow." Kenny shook his head. "This is a load off my mind. I was worried that Howard might actually think about promoting me."

"You don't want a promotion?" April asked, clearly confused.

"Heck, no. I like my job just as it is. I earn a good salary, take long lunches, play some golf. That's plenty for me. Michael here can handle the headaches. He thrives on stress."

"So you're okay with this whole thing? You'll play along?" Michael asked.

"Sure. Sounds like it'll be fun. In fact, I can start the ball rolling tomorrow night. There's a birthday party for Howard's wife at their daughter's house. I'll do what I can to spread the word."

Michael clapped Kenny on the back. "Thanks, buddy. I knew I could count on you. Incidentally, April, if it hadn't been for Kenny here, I never would've found you." April's eyebrows shot up. "He remembered you from when he delivered some paperwork to Web Works."

April nodded. "Yes, I remember." She then narrowed her eyes in a mock glare. "Thanks, Kenny."

He laughed heartily. "Glad I could help. By the way, April, Michael stands to get a handsome promotion out of this. What will you get out of it?"

She tilted her chin up and announced proudly, "Tires."

Chapter Seven

After Kenny left, Michael escorted her to reception, where Shelley still smiled like a fool at April.

"I hope you're feeling better soon."

Completely confused, April was about to question the receptionist, but Michael interrupted. "Don't worry, I'll be home early, darling." He gave her a little hug, his hands lingering on her shoulders until they heard a gruff throat being cleared behind them.

"Well, that's what I like to see, clients treated like family."

Michael laughed, and Shelley shot a cat-that-swallowed-the-canary smile at the distinguished elderly gentleman who approached with a decided air of confidence.

Pulling April close and rubbing her shoulder affectionately, Michael announced, "Howard, I'd like you to meet my wife."

As though she were huddled under a blanket, April only half-heard the shocked response that followed, the questions, the congratulations. Michael briefly explained the quick wedding when they'd been away, how they hadn't made the official announcement yet because they were both still in a daze about it.

"Well, no need to keep such a wonderful event a secret any longer. Why not come to my wife's party tomorrow night, and we'll make it a double celebration?"

"Oh, no, that's not necessary, and it certainly wouldn't be fair to your wife," said Michael.

"Nonsense. She's had more birthdays than she cares to count. She'd be happy to have something take the spotlight away from her."

April tensed against Michael, and he clasped her shoulders re-assuringly. "Um, we sort of had plans, Howard. We haven't had much time together since we've been back. April's been working on a special project at Web Works, and my late hours haven't helped. We wanted this weekend to ourselves."

"I insist," said Howard, issuing a mandate. "You have the rest of your lives to be together." He instructed Shelley to give them the details of the party's place and time. "April, it has been a plea-sure to meet the woman who will set this young man straight." With an all-knowing wink, he turned and left without another word.

"Now what?" April asked.

"I guess we go."

She grunted. "I'm not ready! I can't do this. Michael, you've got to get out of it."

"April, it'll be all right. Just let me do the talking. All you have to do is stand there and look pretty."

"That's a tall order. Looking pretty is not one of my strong points."

He studied her curiously. "You're serious, aren't you? Didn't anyone ever tell you you were pretty?"

She sidestepped toward the elevator and away from the ques-tion. "I'd better get going. I have to find my way to the back of my closet to see if there's anything decent hidden there."

Michael held her arm. "I have a better idea. Let's walk over to the mall and buy you something worthy of a new bride."

"No, I hate shopping. I can never find anything I like."

"Then let me find it. All you have to do is try it on."

"Michael, this isn't going to work. I'm really uncomfortable."

"Stay right there. I'll go lock up my office, and we can leave right now."

Without waiting for her answer, he rushed down the hall and ducked into his office. Uneasy, April glanced over at Shelley, who smiled back.

"Why don't you sit down? You can put your feet up on the coffee table over there."

"No, thanks. I'm fine."

When Michael returned, he waved to Shelley. "See you Monday."

While waiting for the elevator, April whispered, "What is up with Shelley? She treats me like I'm . . . delicate or something."

Michael snuck his arm around her shoulders again and whispered close to her ear, "She thinks you're pregnant."

April's head shot up, and her mouth opened in shock just as the elevator doors opened. Michael pushed her inside before she could voice her alarm within earshot of the receptionist.

"Why does she think that? What did you tell her?"

"I didn't tell her anything. She somehow put things together, erroneously. The quick wedding, the teddy bear balloon. That combined with your uneasiness every time she sees you, I guess she formed a natural conclusion."

"Well, you'd better set her straight before she starts to wonder where the baby is nine months from now."

After a brisk walk, they arrived at the mall. April seldom shopped at the four-story palace of glass and bright lights, since most of the stores were too overpriced for her budget.

Michael quickly steered her into a popular fashion store for women. "Since it's not a formal party, you should be able to find something here. What do you prefer, a dress, skirt, pantsuit?"

April glanced around, lost in the world of coordinated fashion and chic designs. "I'm afraid I'm not very good at this, Michael. Usually if it fits, and the price is right, I buy it."

"Then let's get started. You see if it fits, and I'll say if the price is right."

He circled the racks, picking out several dresses, a pantsuit, and a long skirt. One by one she tried them on and, following his instructions, came out for his inspection. He nodded at a few dresses, frowned at the pantsuit, but gaped speechlessly at the classically styled crimson dress that stopped just above her knees.

"That's it."

Feeling self-conscious, April tugged at the hemline, trying to pull it lower. "Michael, it's too short. I feel . . . overexposed."

"Oh, no, believe me, it's just right." His eyes skimmed her

from top to bottom, then focused on her legs. "You have great legs. They should be seen."

"It's not funny, Michael. I don't wear dresses." She gave the person in the mirror a disapproving look.

Suddenly, he was behind her, his hands on her shoulders, his finger teasing a curl. "Well, you should," he whispered, "because you really do have great legs."

The warmth of his breath near her ear sent chills down her spine. She watched him in the mirror, a vivacious man lavishing attention on a woman she didn't recognize with words she'd never heard.

He seemed preoccupied as he studied her in the mirror. He nudged his cheek against her hair and trailed one hand down her arm. Slowly, the other hand wound around her waist. The pounding in her ears blocked out any words he might have said.

As though thinking better of it, he removed his hand, took a step back, and ran stiff fingers through his hair. "Go get dressed, and I'll look around for shoes and a bag."

He left so quickly, she gulped for air as though it had been sucked right out of her. And then an overwhelming emptiness enveloped her. She was alone in the mirror. She missed his nearness.

By the time she came out of the dressing room, he'd picked out shoes, a matching handbag, and two pairs of shimmering nylons.

"Just try on the shoes, and we can be on our way."

Thankfully, he'd chosen a pair with sensible heels. They felt a bit more cramped than her comfortable clogs, but she really liked the chic style, and she didn't want to disappoint him. He definitely had excellent taste, or at least he knew what he liked his women to wear.

At the cash register, she almost choked when the saleswoman announced the total, but Michael never batted an eyelash. He just plunked down his credit card and grinned at April.

They left, each carrying a bag, and Michael veered into the next store, a men's specialty shop. "I need a new tie. I want you to pick one out."

April gawked at the rows and rows of silks in every color and pattern imaginable while Michael waited for her to choose.

"I—I don't know. There are so many," she whispered.

Seeing her dilemma, he picked out two and held them against his chest. "Which one?"

His broad smile didn't exactly help her concentration. She tried hard to focus on the ties, but her gaze constantly shifted to his face, his hands, his shoulders. She remembered the warmth of him close to her, his scent, and the brush of his whisper against her ear.

"No, wait," he blurted. "Pick up that gray one next to you, the one with the red splashes." She did as he said. "Here, put it between these two." He motioned between the two ties he already held.

Taking an unsteady step forward, April cautiously splayed the tie against his hard but inviting chest. She felt it rise beneath her palm, matching her own intake of breath, and his warm exhale blew against the back of her hand.

"Well?" he asked.

She looked from one tie to another and came to the conclusion that it wouldn't matter what he wore. He was too good-looking for clothes to make a difference.

At that insipid thought, her face heated instantly.

"What? Don't any of them look good?"

She coughed. "Oh, yes, the middle one is great. Yes, that's the one." She lowered the tie.

"Good, because it will match perfectly with your dress."

He immediately went to the cashier while April waited in amazement. He'd picked a tie to go with her dress! Who'd've thought?

They left the store, and April set her course for the street-level exit. But Michael stopped her with a hand on her arm.

"Let's at least get something to eat. It doesn't seem right to keep you so late, then send you home on an empty stomach."

"Oh, I don't mind. It's been a very long week."

"Please have dinner with me. I've enjoyed this, and I'd like it to continue a little longer."

His dark eyes glowed in the glitter and sparkle of the mall's lights. She felt entranced, bewitched, no longer tired. Just being around Michael Goode had revitalized her, and she didn't want it to end either.

"Okay. But nothing fancy. I'm really not dressed for it."

His easy smile spread. The one-dimpled cheek captured her attention, and she smiled back as easily as if they'd known each other forever. She wondered how so much could have happened so quickly. If she wasn't careful, she might find herself liking him.

They walked a few quick steps, when Michael suddenly stopped and backtracked. "Wait, we have to go in here."

He ducked into a store's entrance, and before April realized it was a jewelry store, he'd already made his way to the main counter. She reluctantly followed.

Intently studying the contents of the glass case below him, Michael nodded to the clerk. "Yes, I'd like that wedding band with the row of diamonds for my wife." Behind him, April gasped. He turned to take her hand. "Come here, honey. You have to try it on."

April shook her head slightly but watched in amazement as he tested the ring on her finger. Her eyes must've been stuck open, because she didn't remember blinking.

"No, I'm afraid it's too big. Do you have a smaller size?" He handed the ring back to the clerk, who said they could have it reduced to fit the lady. "No, I want the ring now." The man said he'd check in the back.

When he left, April grabbed Michael's arm. "What are you doing? You can't buy me that ring!"

"Why not?"

"Did you see the price? It's way too expensive."

"April. If you are going to be my wife, you need a wedding ring to make it believable. And anyone who knows me knows that I would lavish my wife with expensive things. So get used to it."

The clerk returned with a velvet tray and a satisfied smile. "I have this one, which is slightly narrower, but it has one more diamond. Would you like to try it?"

Without a word, Michael took the ring from the tray and gently slipped it over April's knuckle. He beamed as he turned the band on her ring finger. "I do believe it's a perfect fit."

He gazed into her eyes, and she gulped for air as her throat tightened with unexpected emotion. "Yes," she whispered, unable to think of anything else to say.

Once again, Michael flashed his credit card and his smile. He pocketed the velvet box the clerk offered. "She'll wear it home."

Handing Michael the receipt, the clerk smiled at both of them. "Congratulations, Mr. and Mrs. Goode."

Michael watched April finish her chop suey. He liked watching her eat. In fact, he liked everything about her. Somewhere between Wednesday and Friday he'd become completely captivated by this creative, witty, unpredictable woman who had an obvious self-esteem problem when it came to relationships.

Ironically, Michael never did. He attracted more women than he needed, picked up any woman with a snap of his fingers, and generally discarded those who no longer suited him. But now, for the first time in his life, he felt he had to work at winning over a woman, and he found the challenge invigorating.

April pushed aside her dish and sat back with a groan. "I'm going to regret this in the morning."

"I hope that doesn't mean me."

She wrinkled her brow for a second, then shook her head. "I meant the food. Chinese makes me bloat something terrible. It's a good thing tomorrow's Saturday, so I can throw on my sweats—oh no, the dress! What if it doesn't fit tomorrow night?"

"Bloating, huh? The best thing I know for serious bloating is to beat the body at its own game. Fight fire with fire."

"What are you talking about?"

"When the body retains water, it's because it thinks it's not going to get any more, so it stores it up for later. What you have to do is drink a lot of water until that little mechanism is triggered, and the water is released. Exercise helps speed it along."

"Do you have a medical degree too?"

He laughed. "Nah, I work out, and you pick up these things along the way. Hey, I have a great idea. When I go for my run in the morning, why don't you join me?"

Her look of distaste nearly wounded his ego, until he realized it was aimed at the activity, not him. "I'm not the running kind, thanks. Flat feet make it difficult. My Saturday exercise consists of running up and down the stairs to take out the trash and do laundry."

Understandable, but he wasn't about to give up. Now that he'd fixed the notion in his head to spend as much time as possible with her, he just needed to figure out how to get her to agree.

"What about biking?"

"Ha! I haven't ridden a bike since . . . high school, I guess. Wow, when I think back, I used to pedal everywhere. Until my junior year."

"When you got your license?"

"No, when I sold my bike because I desperately wanted a pair of designer jeans. My parents couldn't afford them, and I didn't want to wait until Christmas."

Michael laughed. "I know the feeling. I tutored math students just to have spending money for a movie and popcorn."

"You? You mean you didn't have an allowance weighing down your pockets?"

"Go ahead, laugh, but I wasn't always this well off. My dad struggled to keep shoes on me and my older brother. He managed okay being a single dad and a postal worker, but we didn't have many luxuries. My mom died when I was only three, so he spent a lot on babysitters."

She looked at him, wide-eyed. "Gosh, I never would have figured you as working-class offspring."

"Oh, and what do working-class offspring look like?"

"Me. My dad was a floor supervisor in a factory. My mom stayed home but took in sewing jobs—alterations and such. Thank God they had only me, 'cause that shoestring was stretched to its limit."

He saw the sadness in her eyes, the regret that she had missed out on a lot of what other kids had. But then it was gone, as quickly as it'd come. As though she knew that worrying over missed material things was childish.

"So, you don't own a bike anymore, but I do. I could run, and you could bike. What do you say? It'd give us more time to get to know each other, you know, like the couple we're supposed to be."

She wrinkled her nose while playing with the ice in her cup. "I don't know. I sort of had plans to clean my house tomorrow."

"Heck, why stay in and clean when it's supposed to be one of the nicest days we've had so far this spring? Come on, where do you live? We'll meet where it's convenient."

"Pawtucket."

"Perfect. I live in Lincoln. We can meet at the Blackstone Valley bike path at eight."

"Eight? Are you kidding? It's Saturday. Why so early?"

"Nine?"

"Ten."

"Nine thirty."

"All right," she conceded. "But don't expect miracles."

He smiled. As far as he was concerned, the miracle had already happened. "I'll bring the bike and water bottles."

Shaking her head, she rose to gather her things, mumbling all the while. "I can't believe I'm doing this. I can't believe what I've agreed to. Biking. Playing a wife. Dressing up. Jewelry! What next?"

Michael hid a smirk as he followed her out of the food court. He could think of quite a lot to come next, but now wasn't the time to bring it up.

April slammed her hand down on the alarm clock to silence the annoying buzzer.

Eight thirty.

She had to be nuts to agree to Michael Goode's crazy idea. Bike riding? On a Saturday morning? She squinted at the clock to make sure it really read eight thirty. Anything more, she'd be late; anything less, she'd go back to sleep.

Yes, she had to get up despite every instinct that told her she'd regret it. Tired and irritable, she tried to work her way to the edge of the bed. That's when she realized her prediction had come true—the bloating had already begun. One by one, she lowered her heavy legs to the floor and rolled her stiff body out of bed. She stumbled to the bathroom like a whale in search of a beach.

Avoiding the mirror, knowing that puffy eyes would stare back at her, she splashed some water in her face, not entirely certain it would help in her weighted condition. Then, like a woman possessed, she brushed her teeth until her gums ached.

Feeling a little more human, she wrestled her unruly curls into a ponytail and changed into maroon sweats. As soon as she'd gulped down a glass of orange juice, she trudged to her car, mumbling all the way.

Who could bike, much less run, at the crack of dawn? A non-human, that's who. Michael Goode couldn't be human. He was too perfect. Good looks, great physique, charm, finesse, smart, personable. He had to have some faults, one at least.

April, on the other hand, was all faults. Her looks were okay, but her hair was unmanageable. Her figure was better than average, but she disliked her hips. Her social graces were unpolished, leaving her uncomfortable in the presence of strangers. Brains, yeah, she had them, but a degree from a little-known college wasn't anything to brag about, even though it had been all she could afford.

As she pulled into the small lot at the entrance to the bike path, she decided the one thing she had going for her was her personality.

Like when a guy wants to fix up his best friend with a girl who has a great personality. That would be April.

In this instance it didn't really matter, because she wasn't trying to impress Michael Goode. They had an arrangement, that's all. A business deal. She would rely on her personality to get her through this farce and leave her feelings completely out of it.

"Mornin'!" The cheery male voice had the unmistakable stamp of Michael Goode's optimism. "You're late." And his undeniable penchant for detail.

April closed her car door and turned to lock it so she wouldn't have to stare at the muscular arms and chest barely covered by a thin white T-shirt.

"Two minutes, big deal."

"Just two? Hmm, seems longer. But I've been here since nine, warming up."

Naturally. In college he probably read all his books before the semester began. "Well, if you're too tired, we can just forget about the run, then."

His dimple dented deviously. He grabbed her hand and pulled her toward the bike path entrance. "Not a chance. I'm looking forward to this run." He looked down at the hand he held in his. In a low voice, he said, "I see you're wearing your ring."

She felt her cheeks warm. "Your ring, you mean, and no, I wasn't about to leave something this expensive lying around."

The dimple deepened. "Good, that's good. That way you'll get used to wearing it. Here, this is my bike." He lifted a water bottle from a holder on the black crossbar. "Take some long swigs, so your body knows it's not being deprived."

Reluctantly, she grabbed the bottle. "It's being deprived, all right, of sleep!" She gulped down two long swigs, then wiped her mouth against the back of her hand. "Coffee would've been so much better."

Michael replaced the bottle, then hit the kickstand. "Okay, hop on, and let's get going."

With that, he pulled down his warm-up pants, stuffed them into the pack behind the seat, and took off at a brisk pace. April almost fell over the bike as she watched his muscular legs pound the pavement. His calves tightened with the strain; his thighs bulged with each forward stride. As she pedaled furiously to catch up with him, she soon regretted her thick sweatshirt. He wove in and out of the path's traffic. Bikers, walkers, joggers, Rollerbladers. Michael ran, and April barely kept up on the bike. When they reached the three-mile mark, he slowed down, turned to gauge her distance, and waited for her to come alongside.

"How are you making out?"

"Okay," she lied, winded. Michael nodded, blowing out the bad air while jogging in place; she balanced the bike between her legs.

"Take some water, as much as you can."

She did as he said and surprised herself by finishing the bottle with very little effort, but she immediately regretted it when she handed it over and he shook the empty container.

"I'm sorry, I drank it all."

He smiled. "There's more." He went to the bag behind the seat and pulled out another. He gulped most of the contents, then splashed some on his neck.

April watched the water flow down his neck, shoulders, chest, back. She swallowed hard, telling herself to stop staring, then grabbed for the bottle and took another huge drink.

"Warm?" he asked. She nodded, averting her eyes. "Want to take that sweatshirt off?"

She fisted her hands on her hips. "Excuse me, but I'm not an exhibitionist."

His hearty laugh echoed through the woods on either side of them, the greenery waving in agreement. "There's a T-shirt in the bag if you care to wear it."

"Oh." April looked around apprehensively. The coast seemed clear. One jogger appeared about a half mile up, and she saw no one behind them for at least another half mile. With only a moment's hesitation, she pulled the shirt out of the bag and over her head.

Michael's eyebrows shot up with interest.

Returning his half smile with an all-knowing one of her own, she drew her arms out of her sleeves, brought the T-shirt down inside the sweatshirt, and found the arm holes. In seconds, she had the sweatshirt off, replaced by his extra-large shirt, all without baring an ounce of flesh.

"Impressive." He chuckled and turned around to begin the run back.

April stuffed her sweatshirt into the bag and hurried to catch up again. But this time her calves protested in pain after their rest, and her bottom ached from the hard seat. Even her breath became labored more quickly. She easily felt like the biggest wimp, but she wasn't about to complain, or stop.

As they reached the end of the path, Michael bent over, his hands on his knees. He breathed deeply and signaled for April to put the bike off to the side while he walked a few cool-down circles. She waited on unsteady legs.

"So, how do you feel?" he finally asked when his breath evened out.

"Like I have to pee a bucketful."

"Good! See? It worked." He reached for a strand of hair that had escaped her ponytail. "You can go at my place. It's only five minutes from here."

She took the strand from his fingers and tucked it into place. "No, I can make it home."

"What about breakfast? If you haven't eaten, I'd be glad to make you some."

She shook her head. "I'm still stuffed from last night."

He moved closer, and his hand cradled her chin. "Is there anything I can say to entice you to come home with me?"

In the bright sunlight his eyes were clear, light brown, and seductive. His skin glistened from the workout. He leaned closer, barely a breath between them.

Oh, sweet heaven. This kind of thing only happened in movies, certainly not in April's dull life. She watched his mouth lower to hers and remembered its warmth before it even touched.

"No." She jerked her head back just before his lips touched. "I have to get home."

She had to remember, this was not a budding relationship. It was a business deal. To Michael, she wasn't a love interest or even a date. She was an arrangement.

For the first time, Michael looked annoyed, but he quickly masked it by changing the subject. "I'll need your phone number and address for tonight."

"Right." She walked to her car and dug out a pen and scrap of paper to write the information. But before handing it over, she shook her head slowly. "Michael, I don't think I can go through with this charade. I'm not good at acting."

He studied her with a lingering look. "Then don't act. Make it real."

"How? I'm not married to you, so how can it be real?"

He pulled the hem of her T-shirt until they were nose to nose. "You can't deny we have an attraction to each other. It's not an act. Just let go. Ride the emotions wherever they take you. Just because we'll be husband and wife doesn't mean we can't like each other."

A strange analogy, she thought. "Liking you isn't what worries me." What worried her was that he admitted his attraction, yet the charade came first. If she succumbed to the first, she'd regret the latter.

"Nothing about me should worry you, April."

Before she could respond, he took her mouth with a fierceness he hadn't displayed before. Hunger and passion mixed to weaken her resolve. She joined him in the kiss until they had to stop for breath.

He leaned his forehead on hers. "My offer is still open. Breakfast at my house."

With a big intake of breath, she squared her shoulders. "I'll see you tonight."

Chapter Eight

Michael eyed the clock. He didn't want to be late, but he didn't want to show up too early either. She'd said she'd be ready by six. He had ten more minutes.

Checking his tie in the mirror for the tenth time, he shook his head at the sight of the nervous, tightly wound, thirty-six-year-old boy. Where had the self-assured bachelor-for-life gone? Why did this one date matter so much?

He told himself it was the marriage pretense that bothered him, but he knew it had more to do with April's acceptance of it. She'd balked at being with him since the first day they met, yet whenever he kissed her, he felt an instant connection to something he'd never experienced before. An emotion so foreign he couldn't put a label on it. But he liked it, and so did she, apparently, which was why he couldn't refrain from kissing her at every opportunity.

And tonight, he'd see that there was plenty of opportunity. He'd ride this wave wherever it took him.

By the time he pulled his black Corvette in front of April's apartment building, he'd regained his familiar confidence. As he got out of the car, several young neighborhood boys gravitated to the street to get a better look.

"Whoa, man, your car is awesome!"

"Thanks. Hey, what do you guys know about the lady who lives here on the second floor?"

"April? She's cool," said the oldest boy. "She sits on the front steps sometimes and watches us skateboard."

"Yeah," the little one chimed in, "once she even tried it, but she fell off when she hit a dip. She said a *very* bad word."

Michael laughed. "Listen, you guys look pretty sharp. Can you help a dude out? Have you seen her with any boyfriends lately? I mean, what's my competition?"

The older one waved a hand. "Nah, she gets home from work pretty late and stays in. On weekends she runs some errands, sometimes her parents come over for dinner, but that's all. No boyfriends lately."

"Cool." Michael high-fived the boy. "Catch you later."

He approached April's door relieved and relaxed, but when she answered his buzz, all semblance of coherence flew out the window at the sight before his eyes. She'd tamed her blond curls into a perfect frame around her heart-shaped face. With just the right amount of makeup, she'd transformed her pretty features into a vision of beauty. A small gold chain hung from her delicate neck, drawing his eyes downward to her shapely figure. Why hadn't he noticed that before?

Because she'd always been hiding in loose-fitting clothes that gave away nothing. But this crimson dress with the classic lines accented her physical assets, and Michael patted himself on the back for choosing it.

"You look great," he sighed.

"I still feel bloated."

"You'd never know it from looking at you."

"Just don't let me eat anything salty."

They left the apartment and walked to the street, where the boys still huddled around the Vette. April sucked in her breath. "Is *this* your car?"

He nodded. "My weakness. I collect toys."

He held the door open as she folded herself into the car and swung her legs in. Michael glanced down. *My newest weakness— your legs.*

They arrived at the Narragansett home of Howard Gellar's daughter as the sun dipped low in the sky and twilight painted magical colors on the ocean beyond. Sounds of the surf could be heard beyond the music and laughter coming from within the great stone house.

Michael removed April's shawl, gingerly touching her exposed neck and delighting in her quick intake of breath. Bending his head close, he whispered, "You really do look fantastic."

She blushed appreciatively.

He handed her shawl to an attendant in the foyer, then took April's arm to lead her to the lively reception in the large room to their right. Michael removed a small gift package from his jacket and placed it with others on a corner table hosting a huge birthday cake.

"Well, well, well. If it isn't Mr. and Mrs. Goode," Kenny Gellar loudly proclaimed as he made his way toward them, drink in hand. "You two look like the perfect married couple."

"Keep it down, Kenny. *Mrs.* Goode is still getting used to the idea." He held a reassuring grip on April's hand and lowered his eyebrows menacingly at his co-worker.

Kenny tilted his head in acknowledgment. "Sorry, my dear." He reached for her free left hand. "You look absolutely stunning." When she laughed, he bent to kiss her hand but stopped and let out a low whistle. "Well, will you look at that ring! I see *Mr.* Goode is very serious about this marriage."

Michael felt April stiffen next to him. "All right, Kenny, you've had your fun. Go bother someone else for a while."

"I've already bothered everyone here."

"Then go spend some time with *your* wife."

With a shrug and a wink at April, Kenny moved along.

She sighed heavily. "Michael, I feel so foolish here. I don't know anyone."

He tugged her hand closer. "You know me, and that's all that matters."

"But what if they're all like Kenny, if they all think it's a big joke?"

"They won't. Trust me. Now, let's blend in."

Before long, they'd circled the room, greeting Gellar family members and a few business associates. Michael did all the talking, but April got all the stares, especially after he introduced her as his wife. She stood out like a cherry atop an ice cream sundae, and in his dark suit, Michael was the chocolate sauce wrapped around her.

When dinner was announced, they found their seats at the

opposite end of the huge table from Howard Gellar. Lively conversations buzzed all around, but Michael concentrated on April. He ate most of the meal with his head turned to the right, devouring her beauty and drinking in her excitement.

"Michael, I can't believe I'm sitting at a table with an ex-governor."

"Sweetie, the Gellars know everyone in Rhode Island. Word has it he never would've been elected in the first place if it hadn't been for Howard Gellar."

"What about his daughter's husband—what does he do? I mean, this house is unbelievable."

"Funny thing, no one really knows." Michael laughed behind his napkin. "Some things are best left unknown."

"I feel so out of place."

"You're not. Look around. You've gotten more admiring glances this evening than even the guest of honor."

"Because you introduced me as your wife, and they can't believe you chose me."

Michael lowered his hand to hers and rubbed his pinky finger along hers. "No, they can't believe I finally found someone to tame me."

She turned a saucy smile on him. "Oh? You need taming?"

"I'm not saying I need it, but you're welcome to try."

She giggled. "And here I thought I was the one being tamed."

Michael nuzzled her shoulder. "You can be as wild as you want with me." His sly wink caused her to laugh a little too loudly. A few guests turned.

At the head of the table, Howard Gellar stood, tapping his wineglass to gain everyone's attention. "I'd like to thank you all for coming to celebrate this wondrous night with my family. My wife has given me strict instructions not to reveal her age, so let's just say she's old enough to know better but young enough not to care."

Laughter rolled up and down the table, and Connie Gellar blushed like a woman half her age.

"So, I'd like to propose a toast to the woman who's made my life complete, who blessed me with this lovely daughter, who in turn holds my heart hostage with *her* daughter. What else can I say? I love all the women in my life."

He held up his wineglass, and everyone toasted to the Gellar women.

"And now, there's one more special announcement tonight. Most of you know Michael Goode from my firm. Michael is the image of myself at that age—well, he might be a bit better-looking than I was." More laughter rang out. "In any case, he has the drive and the vitality I remember back then, and without him for the past few years, I don't know if Gellar would be where it is today—at the top of the investment game!" Applause split the air.

"Because of that, it's my great pleasure to announce his recent marriage. I want to wish him and his lovely wife, April, all the best and many, many years of happiness."

Again the toasts rang out, and Michael nodded to all the well-wishers. Then someone tapped a glass with a spoon, and others joined in until the clinking of glasses became deafening. He had no choice but to oblige the tradition. He turned to April, whose eyes were as wide as her dinner plate, and greedily kissed the lips he'd wanted for the past hour.

When the applause erupted, he lifted his head and smiled into her stunned blue eyes.

"That was delicious."

It was almost nine thirty by the time the last course had been cleared and two waiters rolled in the towering cake for Mrs. Gellar to cut. Like a kid, Michael dug into his cake topped with a double scoop of ice cream. April laughed as he licked the last of the creamery from his lips. She couldn't ever remember having this much fun on a date.

"You missed a spot," she murmured, and she leaned forward to dab her napkin just above his chin.

Their eyes locked, and for the first time Michael Goode seemed speechless. A flutter in April's stomach grew stronger with every passing moment of his intense gaze. She found she enjoyed his company, the attention he paid her, and the way he made her feel important. He wasn't the ogre she'd first thought, or the self-centered egomaniac. Even though this was all a sham, she was proud to be his wife for the night.

He leaned closer. "Let's go out on the terrace where we can talk."

April rose to follow him out the French doors, but before they got halfway across the room, Howard Gellar stopped them.

"Michael, April, I have something I want to give you." He reached into his coat pocket and handed over a business card with a large gold *G* insignia in the center and a small etching of a boat in an upper corner.

April peeked over his shoulder, trying to read the small print, while Michael, clearly puzzled, stared at the card. He looked up at his boss with genuine surprise.

"What's this?"

"It's a card with the name and location of our yacht in Newport. We're heading out to sea the weekend after next for a few days, and we'd love for you to join us. Consider it an extended honeymoon."

April looked at Michael. This couldn't be. Surely he would say something, something kind but noncommittal. A weekend on a boat—as a couple—was out of the question.

"Well, thank you, sir. That is most generous."

Aghast, April turned to Michael. "No, we can't."

His head shook so slightly, April almost missed it. "Why not, dear? Because of that dinner party? It was canceled, remember? Our schedule is clear."

She thought about stomping on his foot or maybe elbowing him in the ribs. But that would be childish and too obvious. "Yes, I did forget. But something tells me we still can't go. . . ."

"Now, now," Gellar patronized, "I'm sure if you can't remember, then it can't be that important. What's important when starting out in marriage is that you're together and that you enjoy yourselves. I would consider it a personal honor to have you with us for the weekend."

Gellar's hand clasped April's. She gulped. What could she say? He was so kind, so generous, so firmly planted in family values. April hated that they were deceiving him.

"Thank you, Mr. Gellar. It would be our pleasure."

"Howard, call me Howard. I may be old, but I still think young!" With a rumble of laughter, he moved off to strike up a conversation on the other side of the room.

In a flash, April tugged Michael out to the terrace. "You've *got* to get us out of that!"

"But you just told him it would be our pleasure."

"What else was I supposed to say? Did you want me to tell him the truth? 'No, we can't go because we're not really married.' Get real, Michael. This sham is going to come back to bite us."

Michael reached for her shoulder, but she pulled away. "April, you're overreacting. I know you're feeling guilty because Howard's a nice guy, but, honest, I can handle this."

"And what if he finds out you scammed him *after* you get the promotion? Do you really want to chance losing his respect? My God, Michael, he looks upon you like a proud father. The disappointment would kill him."

For the first time, she saw remorse on Michael's face. His eyes lost some of their glimmer. "I know, I thought about that. But I can't stop it now. I'd look so stupid, and, well . . ." He edged closer and reached for her hand. "I'm sort of enjoying this." His finger rubbed her wrist. "You've made it an adventure I look forward to each day. How can a little cruise hurt?"

She reached into his other hand and pulled out the card. "This is how. This cruise means we have to act as a married couple, staying in one room and, I'd venture to say, one bed. That's not in our marriage contract."

He stilled her hand as she waved the card under his nose and caught her off-guard with a tempting kiss. "Then let's renegotiate."

Because she was too surprised to fight it, he pulled her to his chest and planted a slow, meaningful kiss on her silenced lips. April knew she should fend him off, but his kiss was too tempting, his scent too intoxicating, his words too stimulating.

And as she leaned into him, she knew that fending off this man would not come easily.

He wanted her.

Michael pulled April closer with a need he didn't know existed.

He wanted her, wanted to know what went on in that pretty little head, what ingrained values held her back from him.

He knew enough about women to know she found him attractive. Her appreciative glances, her body language, her eagerness when they kissed. But she held back from anything more, and he had to find out how to unleash the real woman who certainly lived within.

She suddenly pulled back and tapped the card against his chest. "There's no need to renegotiate. Our agreement was that I pretend to be your wife for social functions. The cruise is a social function. The sleeping arrangements are not. You have to get us out of this—that's all there is to it."

Frustration weighed heavily in every part of his body. He leaned his forehead against hers and struggled to regain his composure. Taking the card from her cold fingers, he slipped it into his pocket.

"You don't have to do anything you don't want, I mean, with the sleeping arrangements. I'd never do that to you. But this opportunity is very important to me, and not just because the boss invited us. I really want to spend time with you, April. I'll sleep on the floor if I have to, but I'd never force my way into your bed. That's not my style."

She relaxed against his chest. He felt the tension flow out of her like the air from an unplugged water raft, and her fingers grew warm again in the hand he'd reclaimed. His assurance had worked; she no longer felt pressured. With that realization, Michael threw strategy out the window and set his mind to showing April the real Michael Goode.

But did he even know himself? As a scared adolescent, he'd tried to skip school to avoid taking part in his first debate. But his father had bolstered his confidence with the simple statement that everyone had insecurities. The secret was to discover the other guy's before he discovered yours.

This past week had been a series of self-discoveries for the now self-assured, self-proclaimed bachelor. The mere idea of marriage had shaken him to the core when he'd first been confronted with the fake wedding album. But once he'd met April, the reason for his insecurity didn't matter. He liked being with her. He liked her refreshing look at the world and at him.

She was so unlike other women he dated, some picture-perfect models, that he began to wonder what he had ever seen in the dull, selfish beauties he collected like artwork to hang on his wall. April wasn't meant to be hung on a wall. She deserved to be taken down, held, appreciated. Her beauty began within and blossomed without when handled properly.

By him.

She stirred in his arms. "I appreciate your honesty, Michael."

With a hooked finger, he lifted her chin till her eyes met his. "So, we've got a date, then?"

The slightest glimmer of hesitation sparked in her eyes, then vanished, leaving a hopeful gleam. A quick nod was followed by a half smile.

"Okay. But I'm not promising I'll be the best of company. I'm afraid I'll be too focused on acting like a wife."

He wrapped her in an embrace. "Just be yourself. It'll be more than enough."

She loved being in his arms.

Michael Goode had surprised her with attentiveness and tenderness during an evening expected to be nerve-shattering. True to his word, he'd watched out for her, done all the talking, smoothed the way. He'd been like a hero in a romantic movie.

But was it all an act? Were his attentions merely for the benefit of the crowd or a ploy to make her relax in her role? She didn't want to believe that was the case, but she cautioned herself to the possibility.

Don't get sucked in. The fall could be hard. The pain of Stan's disappointment still lingered in her bruised heart.

Michael finally eased his hold around her, reluctantly, it seemed. Taking her hand, he guided her to the railing overlooking the starlit ocean surf.

"Now, tell me why a smart, pretty girl like you doesn't have a boyfriend."

She threw him an amused look. "How do you know I don't?"

"I have my sources."

"How dare you sneak around checking up on me. . . . Wait, it was the boys at my building, wasn't it?"

Michael chuckled. "Hey, us guys stick together on stuff like that. They knew it was important information."

"Why?"

"I had to know if I had any competition."

"You're not competing for anything. We're only pretending we're a couple." It helped to remind herself of that often, knowing how weak she was in the self-discipline department.

"Right." He looked away for a moment, then turned back. "Don't you want to ask about me?"

"Ask what?"

"If I'm seeing anyone?"

The burning question had popped into her head more than once. With those looks and that charm, he could have any woman he wanted, and some he didn't want. Throw in the money, the car, the position—well, the list could be endless.

"Again, what does it matter? I'm not competing for you."

"Mmm," he mumbled. His lips formed a tight line, and the dimple had disappeared without a trace. "Well, I'm not. Seeing anyone," he added dramatically.

For some strange reason, that admission made her ecstatically happy. April fought the smile that pulled at her lips. Her mother would be proud of her.

"And do you want to know why?" he continued, his voice bold with emphasis.

"No."

"Because so many of the women I date are boring. They have no thoughts of their own. Everything centers on what I think, how I feel. If I asked them to jump off a cliff with me, they'd say 'Okay' and do it."

She turned her attention to the ocean. "I thought men liked a certain amount of adoration from women."

"I did too, once. It just became so monotonous. I felt that every woman I dated was the same as the last. Right off the assembly line."

"Then why did you keep doing it? Why didn't you pick from a different factory?"

She felt his strong hand on her shoulder, turning her toward him. The sound of the ocean suddenly swelled louder inside her head, rushing past her ears. When their eyes met, she saw what looked like the uncertainty of a young boy dealing with oncoming adulthood.

"You're not like them, April. You have thoughts, you have feelings, and you're not the least bit boring."

She laughed nervously. "Try talking to me after I've been at the computer for ten hours straight."

"Stop putting yourself down. Why do you always belittle yourself?"

April started to answer, then stopped. Michael's intense gaze searched her eyes for something, but she didn't know what. What did he hope to find hidden inside her?

"Do I? I guess it's just a habit, certainly not something I do consciously."

His hands loosened on her shoulders. He seemed to relax, and his eyes warmed with a comforting glow. "Well, when you're with me, you don't need to, because it won't work. No wife of Michael Goode would put herself down." The dimple slowly crept back as he inched forward.

"I'm not your wife, Michael."

Ignoring her remark, he pulled her closer and kissed her fervently. She felt his heart beating between them. It managed to set off a stirring deep within her that short-circuited any coherent thought she might have had. She circled her arms tightly about his neck. Her whole body responded as though a torch had ignited in her veins.

Michael sighed as a moan escaped his throat. He moved away and planted a sweet kiss in her hair.

Lifting his head, he whispered, "Let's get out of here."

Chapter Nine

After politely bidding their hosts good night, Michael ushered April out to the car like an overanxious prom date. His movements were swift, his purpose unmistakable.

But with each step she took away from the elegant house and closer to Michael's extravagant car, April's racing pulse slowed enough to allow some semblance of reason to return. A little voice told her that what had just happened in there had been a reaction to the swirling events of the last few days. Michael Goode had swept her up with his whirlwind optimism. He'd sold her on the idea of a convenient marriage and how easy it would be to pull off.

And they had, tonight. Everyone in there, with the exception of Kenny Gellar, believed they were married and had a long, happy life ahead of them. The problem was, it appeared that Michael had gotten caught up in it too. How far did he expect the pretense to go? Was he really interested in her or just the "wife" he'd created? And did he think she'd fall for the romancing part and become another notch on his belt?

Sadly enough, it was almost true. Tonight had been one of the most exciting dates she'd ever had. Physical attraction aside, she felt they connected on an intellectual level as well. He welcomed her opinions. He listened to her observations.

But his magnetism had taken her by storm. A man like Michael didn't play for the sake of the game. He played to win. By his own admission, women usually did anything he wanted.

"Michael," she blurted as she stopped just feet from the car. Hand hovering over the door handle, he waited. "What are we doing?"

He frowned. His hand returned to his side. "Doing? I thought we were leaving so we could be alone. That's usually what 'Let's get out of here' means."

"In the literal sense, yes, that's what is happening. But in general terms, what are we doing? Do we want to deceive that nice old man? Do we want to fool everyone we work with into thinking we're happily married, when a year down the road they'll be more disappointed in our breakup than we will? And do we want to torment ourselves with a meaningless relationship?"

She saw him struggle for answers to her rhetorical questions. Perhaps *meaningless* was enough for him; maybe it always had been. Could that be why he went from one relationship to another, no one woman more important than the next?

He turned to face her fully, a trace of disappointment saddening his eyes. How do you know it would be meaningless? Are you saying you don't like being with me?"

"No, I—" She looked down for a moment. "What I meant was, we're not a couple. We had no prior relationship. This awkward arrangement brought us together, and to confuse it as real would be a mistake. I take any relationship I have with a man very seriously. I don't think a phony wedding ring or the promise of a set of tires is enough to change the basis of the arrangement."

If she hadn't looked down, she might not have seen his clenched hands pressed against his sides. And if the silence hadn't been so acute, she might not have heard his heavy intake of air.

But when she looked up, his face had remained as calm as if he were in the middle of an investment negotiation. He was strategically sizing up the barriers to assess his alternatives. No wonder the man was so successful.

"The basis of this arrangement hasn't changed. I want that promotion; you owe me a favor. I didn't think it would be a national crisis if we got to know each other in the process."

He turned to the car, opened her door, and gave her a wide berth by gallantly stepping aside. Too unsure of herself to answer his point-blank remark, she slid past him and into the sinfully sleek car. He slammed the door as soon as she'd tucked her foot inside, then stomped to his side of the car.

It was going to be a long ride home.

He drove too fast. He knew it.

Not just because April sat stiffly beside him without uttering a word. Not just because his speedometer read eighty. But because he whizzed by every other car on the road, rendering them mere blurs.

He eased off the gas and slowed to sixty-five. Venting his anger wasn't worth a speeding ticket or risking their lives. It certainly wasn't worth alienating April because she saw the relationship more clearly than he did.

Yes, she'd been right. They were a couple only because he'd forced his way onto her good side, tricking her into believing she owed him this much.

But it was no longer all about the promotion. Heck, he would never have admitted he needed someone else to help him succeed. He was the golden boy, the investment whiz to be reckoned with. Nothing stood in his way when he wanted something badly enough.

April.

That's what he wanted now more than anything. But bullying his way through her defenses wouldn't get him any closer. She had to be won over gently, carefully. And he had to convince her that the promotion was second on his mind.

He pulled up in front of her apartment building and got out. As he came around to her door, she'd already let herself out.

"Thanks, but I think we should say good night here." Her hand clutched her shawl tightly.

"April, I thought about what you said, and you were right."

She raised her eyebrows and lifted the shawl higher over her shoulders. "About what?"

"About us not really being a couple. I can see how you'd feel that way."

"So we can call off all the 'couple' stuff and just be married in name, for Gellar's sake?"

"No, I think we shouldn't worry about the marriage arrangement and just be ourselves."

"I can't do that!"

"Why not?"

"Because . . . it wouldn't be right."

"April." He stepped forward and placed his hands on her shoulders. She stiffened instantly. "April, listen to yourself. You're a bundle of contradictions. You don't want to get involved because we're pretending to be married. You don't want to pretend to be married because we might hurt other people. And you don't want a meaningless relationship because . . . why?"

Her face paled under the blue haze of the streetlight. Her lips worked at forming the right words.

"Because I like you."

Michael dropped his hands from her frozen shoulders and stepped back. She liked him? She was admitting that she really liked him? It sounded like such a minuscule thing, but knowing her as he did, it was monumental. She'd reluctantly agreed to this arrangement with the emphasis that it meant nothing and that when it was all over, it was over. More than once she'd adamantly reminded him it meant nothing.

So now, admitting that she liked him, well, that had to have taken a lot of courage and a lot of pride-swallowing.

He smiled, a little too broadly but securely hidden in the shadow of the light pole. "Good, because I like you too. So why is this a problem?"

"Because I don't want either of us to get hurt when this is over, after you get your promotion."

"And what if I said I didn't care about the promotion?"

"I wouldn't believe you."

He laughed. "You're right. See? You already know me better than I do. But, truthfully, I don't want the original intent of our arrangement to get in the way of us. I really want to get to know you."

She looked down at her feet. "I don't know how to answer that."

He moved closer, reaching for her hand, pulling her to him. "Just say you won't worry about pretending and relax and be yourself."

The brief shadow of a smile skidded across her lips. "Be myself. You might be surprised at the real me."

His hand came up to her face, caressing it gently. "I like surprises."

When her lips parted, it was more than he could stand. He lowered his mouth to take hers, feeling the cool night air warm as their lips joined. Her hands bashfully came up to circle his neck, resting tentatively at the collar of his jacket. But suddenly, with obvious abandon, her fingers delved into his hair, sending an awakening message to his entire body.

And that was his moment of enlightenment.

April was a passionate, caring woman who wanted and felt more than she could admit. Or, rather, she worked at hiding it. He knew he'd have to figure out a way to loosen whatever restraints she'd placed on her emotions, because if nothing else, he was certain that she wanted him.

Lifting his head, he gazed into her glistening eyes. "If that's a hint at the real you, then I think I'll look forward to the rest."

"Maybe that's all there is," she teased.

He tapped her nose. "Oh, no, I'm not that naive. There's a whole lot more to discover, and I can't wait. Tonight we've both learned that we like each other. For now, let's not complicate it beyond that."

April awoke early Sunday morning, unusual for her on a day off. Sundays were for staying under the covers, drifting in and out of dreamland and not thinking.

But today, the day after her first day as a "wife," instead of rolling over and going back to sleep, she slid out of bed and stretched a welcome to the incoming sunshine.

A smile eased across her lips, and warmth spread through her as she thought of her evening with Michael, the "husband." She'd enjoyed herself more than she could have imagined and felt a twinge of remorse that she wouldn't see him that day.

The phone rang, and, as though answering her wish, Michael's cheery, soothing voice greeted her with sugar. "Good morning, darling. Sorry if I woke you."

April laughed at the halfhearted apology. "No, you're not, and no, you didn't."

"Really? I thought you liked to sleep in on weekends."

"I do. But I just woke up early and decided to stay up. I have a lot to do today."

"How about starting the day with me? Join me on my run again?"

She groaned just thinking of the torturous workout he'd put her through yesterday. Her overworked, underused muscles still ached.

"Sorry. Two days in a row might set off rebellious counteractions in my body. I need it to function without argument this week."

His chuckle tickled in her ear. "Okay, then meet me for breakfast."

As good as it sounded, she forced herself to decline. "I can't. I really have a lot of laundry and other things to do before I visit my parents for dinner."

His silence chilled her for a moment until he finally relented with a sigh. "Can't blame a guy for trying. I guess I'll see you at work tomorrow, then."

"Doubtful. I have a new project to start on, and I'll be submerged in Web-design hell all day."

"Not even lunch?"

"Michael, please, don't push it. Like you, I have a job I care about. I need to concentrate on laying the groundwork for this project without interruption. Maybe later in the week we can meet up."

"I'm going to hold you to that."

His warning brought a smile to her lips. "Until then, I need my space."

"Then I'll see you soon."

She couldn't help a forlorn sigh after he hung up. If only this could be a real romance. Because so far it was everything she'd imagined a romance could be.

April's upbeat mood followed her all day and continued as she helped her mother set the food on the table.

"You seem to be in a good mood," her mother noted. "Is it this new guy you met?"

No sense trying to hide the obvious, she thought, and she smiled. "We went out last night to a magnificent party at a beautiful estate in Narragansett. It was actually a business gathering for him, but it felt like a date."

"Oh, let's sit, and you can tell us all about it while we eat." As always, her mother thrived on all things romantic.

April sat down opposite her father, who frowned at the idea of hearing details of his daughter's date. But he needn't worry. She had no intention of giving a play-by-play.

"There isn't much to tell. Like I said, it was more of a business event. We ate a lot, talked to other guests, then left."

"Then why are you so . . . so radiant?"

April felt her face grow warm at the obvious effect Michael Goode had on her. "I guess because Michael has a way of making me feel special."

"Michael? He's the new guy?"

"Yes. Now that's all I'm going to say about it."

"When will we get to meet him? I'd like to see this man who's made you come alive after all this time. You haven't glowed this much since—"

"Don't say it, Mom. Ancient history, remember?" As if she needed to be reminded of Stan. Seeing him Friday was bad enough. And to think she'd almost fallen under his spell again.

They ate the rest of the meal talking about the usual topics, her father much more comfortable joining in on political discussions. When April helped her mother clean up the dishes, their idle chatter came to a halt at the sound of the doorbell. Moments later, her father appeared at the kitchen door with a deathly pale expression on his face.

"April. Can you come out here?"

She quickly wiped her hands on a towel and followed him to the living room. There, big as life, stood her worst nightmare. Stan.

Behind her, her mother stifled a gasp. "Stan. Oh, my."

"Hello, Mrs. Vaillancourt. You're looking wonderful."

"Oh, thank you, yes . . . I . . . um—"

"What do you want?" April cut in.

Stan smiled, that evil, cynical smile that said he was hiding something. He craned his neck, pretending he was trying to look into the kitchen.

"Just you three here?"

In that moment, April knew exactly what he was up to. The lie had come back to bite her already. She turned and quickly handed the towel to her mother.

"I'll be right back."

She lunged for the door, pushing Stan out ahead of her, but not quickly enough.

"Where's Michael? No husband tonight?"

She slammed the door and turned a deadly glare on Stan. "What do you think you're doing? Why did you come here, and how did you know I was here?"

His evil laugh stirred a sour taste inside her. "You're a creature of habit, April. Just like I knew you'd still be working for Tim, I knew I'd find you at your parents' on a Sunday evening. I must say, Michael Goode was a bit of a surprise, though."

"Yeah, my taste has improved."

"Now, April, don't be bitter. I would have given you a good life, nice things. You were just too impatient."

" 'Impatient'? No word from you for months on end, then you'd show up with more promises and leave just as quickly. Year after year, always the same scenario. Did we ever spend any holidays together?"

"I was making a name for myself."

"I have a name for you, but I doubt you'd want it on a business card."

"Look, I didn't come here to fight."

"Then why did you come?"

"Let's just say I had a curious hunch. I drove by and thought it odd that your car was here. By the way, how long have you had that old clunker?"

"Like you said, my habit is to have dinner with my parents on Sunday nights."

"But why aren't you home with your husband, or why isn't he here with you?"

"That's none of your business."

"Honeymoon over already? Or did you even have one to begin with?"

A seething hatred built up inside her until she had to clench her teeth to keep it in. She couldn't tell him the truth, but she couldn't create a bigger lie either. Most of all, she had to keep this whole mess from her parents. They'd brought her up with strong values and taught her not to lie.

"My relationship with Michael is private. I don't have to explain anything to you."

"Why didn't you say your 'marriage to Michael' instead of relationship? Seems an odd way to talk about your husband. Or is he your husband?" He glanced down. "Funny, I still don't see a ring on your finger."

Cornered. She wanted to be honest and say no, they weren't married, just lay out the truth and be done with it. But Stan had already talked about meeting with Michael in his office. What if Stan told Michael she had denied it? What if he talked to someone else in the office? She couldn't let this irksome worm ruin Michael's career.

"Yes, he's my husband." She gulped hard enough to swallow her tongue. "And I must've left my ring near the shower." In fact, it sat in her purse after she'd jerked it off her finger seconds before entering her parents' house.

"Didn't see it on you Friday either. Awfully forgetful about an important piece of jewelry, aren't you?"

That's right. Michael had bought her the ring Friday night, after her run-in with Stan. "I'm not used to wearing it, so I forget sometimes."

"Hmm." Stan stepped forward and placed his hands on her shoulders. "I've never known you to lie, April, so I'll take that as the truth. But there's something suspicious about this, and I plan to find out what it is."

He kissed his finger and touched it to her lips, then left. She swiped the transferred kiss away as though it might contaminate her mouth and stared as he drove off. The adrenaline slowly worked its way out of her system, leaving her with the shakes and a sense of foreboding. Nothing good had ever come out of knowing Stan Tragar.

She finally went inside to face the inevitable interrogation.

"What was that about?" asked her anxious mother. "Is Stan gone?"

"Yes, Mom, he's gone—forever, I hope."

April picked up where she'd left off, drying and stacking dishes, but her mother fidgeted with rinsing and re-rinsing the pans. In a matter of minutes she nearly burst with the obvious question.

"What was that comment about Michael and a husband?"

With a weary sigh, April quickly recapped what had happened at work on Friday. How Stan showed up, Tim worried about her and called Michael, who ran interference by pretending to be her husband. When she'd finished, she was quite proud that she'd spun the tale with no intentional deceit on her part.

"I hope this Michael realizes he ruined your chances with Stan."

"Mom! I don't want a chance with Stan. It's over. It took me a long time to realize it, but he's not the right man for me."

"Is Michael?"

In a different time, a different place, maybe. But for now, all they had between them was a bargain. If she held up her end, he'd hold up his. She wondered how long her strength could last.

"It's not that kind of relationship, Mom. There may never be a right man for me. Maybe my ideals are too high. Or maybe I've seen one too many romantic movies."

Her mother touched her hand and kissed her cheek. "There is a man out there for you, and he'll find you when you least expect it."

Yeah. But was Michael that man?

Chapter Ten

Despite her request that he give her some space, the first thing April saw as she pulled into the parking garage on Monday morning was Michael Goode. His tall, trim figure, handsomely cut in a dark gray suit, leaned against a pillar near the entrance. He straightened as she pulled in and casually walked over.

Holding her door open, he stepped aside until she clumsily got out, dragging a tote bag, briefcase, and large takeout coffee.

"Can I help you with anything?"

She shoved the door with her hip, jerking back as the coffee sputtered from the plastic opening. "I can manage. What are you doing here, anyway? I thought I told you I needed to concentrate on work."

"You're not working yet. Besides, wouldn't it be natural for a husband and wife to arrive together if they work in the same building?"

Was it just her imagination, or did all the men she meet have this penchant for assuming they knew what was in her best interests and that they had the right to direct it? Rolling her eyes, April began walking toward the exit.

"I doubt anyone is watching for that." Her pace quickened when she hit the sidewalk, and she heard him fall into step to match hers.

"How was dinner with your parents?"

She stopped to look him square in the face. "Why?" Did he know something? Had Stan gotten to him too?

His innocent shrug assured her it was nothing of the sort. "Just curious. Idle conversation."

She continued to walk. "No different than usual. Dad complained about the latest corruption scandal in the statehouse, and Mom complained about her favorite department store closing down. Very boring dinner conversation."

"Did you tell them about me?"

April almost tripped on a crack in the sidewalk. "No. Why would I do that?"

"I don't know, just thought you might want to mention a new son-in-law."

"Not funny."

He laughed. "Maybe not, but it would've livened up the conversation, don't you think?"

"That it would." She forced a laugh. She could just envision Dad's sigh of relief that he didn't have to pay for a wedding and Mom's distress that she didn't get to plan one.

But no, thanks to Stan, the night had ended in turmoil, and April had gone home with a splitting headache.

"Say, what time are you getting out?"

"I have no idea. This project is monumental. I'll only stop when I feel I have a handle on where I'm going with it."

"I can wait in my office until you're ready. Just call up, and I'll meet you when you're done so we can leave together."

She shook her head. "No, it could be very late; all depends on how much I accomplish. I don't want to feel pressured, knowing you're waiting for me."

"I understand. But if you happen to finish earlier, just give me a jingle."

They'd reached the entrance to their building, and April went directly to the elevator. Before she could juggle her coffee with her bags, Michael handily pushed the button for her floor. They rode up in silence, but she felt his eyes on her the whole way.

As soon as the car stopped and the doors slid open, Michael planted himself in front of the opening and gripped her shoulders. Before she could ask what he was doing, he leaned over and kissed her surprised mouth. He then released her and stepped aside.

"Have a good day."

April left the elevator, and the doors quickly closed with Michael behind them. But to her side stood Tim Houghton, eyes wide, mouth agape, finger poised over the Down button.

"What a difference a day makes . . . or two."

April leveled a warning glare at her boss, then headed for her office. "It's not what it looks like."

"No?" Tim followed and stepped ahead to push the door open. "As an admitted computer geek, I may be out of touch sometimes, but a kiss is hard to misinterpret."

She dropped her belongings at her desk and turned in exasperation. "Tim, please. I don't have the concentration to explain everything right now. I want to get this Web Galleria project off to a clean start. Don't muddy my brain stirring it for details."

Knowing April worked in a linear, full-steam-ahead fashion, Tim backed off, his hands raised in surrender. "I'm just running down for coffee. Can I get you anything? Danish, juice, hotel room?"

She threw a pencil at him as he dashed out the door, his laugh echoing in the corridor.

When the phone rang shortly after six, April wasn't all that surprised to hear Michael's voice.

"Hi. I'm not calling to bug you. I just wanted to see if you're still working or if you're ready to head home."

She hesitated at the tempting invitation, then answered in a weary tone. "I'm still at it, but I've made progress. I'll be here another hour or two."

"Can I bring you anything? I'd be happy to run down and grab a burger for you."

"Thanks, but Tim already did, and it's sitting here half-eaten on my desk. I'm too tired to eat. I just want to finish up and go home to bed."

"Okay, I'll leave you alone. But, April, I want you to know what a great time I had Saturday night at the party."

"A great time" didn't come close to describing how she felt about it. She'd played the night over and over again in her mind a hundred times like a favorite movie. Pausing on the romantic scenes, reciting the dialogue. After a while, it almost seemed like it *was* a movie, that it had happened to someone else.

In a way it had. It happened to the fictitious wife of Michael Goode. She had to be careful to remember fictitious characters didn't come to life.

"Yes, the Gellars know how to throw a party."

He laughed. "That's not what I meant, but, yeah, it was a great party. And I know I'm keeping you from your work. Good night, April. I'll wait for you in the morning."

She gently replaced the phone and sighed. A dream come true sure would be nice.

True to his word, Michael met her in the garage again the next morning, and the next. He went all out to make a good show of this marriage thing, even though they'd only seen one person from his office the whole time.

By Wednesday, she had enough of the Web Galleria project laid out to allow a little breathing room in her schedule. She agreed to meet Michael for lunch in the food court.

"For a change, we're meeting here under normal circumstances," he said as he poured dressing over his salad.

"Define *normal*."

"Well, the first time I was trying to trip you up to see what you knew about the mysterious wedding album."

She rolled her eyes. "Don't remind me."

"And the second time I was trying to save you from the clutches of that Stan character."

"I repeat, don't remind me."

He dug into his salad and took a few bites before pausing to study her. She sensed an impending ominous moment.

"April, Stan made an appointment with me this afternoon. He says it's for investment advice. He bragged about his fast-lane career, and he wants to put his excess money to good use. But I'm not so sure that's his true motive, or at least all of it."

She shoved her salad aside and rested her head in her hands. "It's not. He suspects."

"Suspects what?"

"That we're not really married." She kept her voice low from possible eavesdroppers.

"How do you know this?"

She sat back. "He came to my parents' house Sunday night and asked a lot of questions. He brought up the ring thing."

"You had it on this time, right?"

"Of course not. I was at my parents' house!"

Michael sat forward, his voice edgy and anxious. "Why didn't you tell me this before?"

"There was nothing you could have done. Don't worry, I took care of it and sent him packing."

"Took care of it how?"

She pulled at her napkin until the paper tore in a jagged line. "I told him it was none of his business, that you were my husband."

"What did your parents say?"

"They didn't hear. We were outside. But my mother asked a lot of questions afterward, and I really didn't like deceiving her like that."

He put his hand over hers, saving the napkin from further annihilation. "I know you don't. I'm sorry you had to go through that—alone. At least you got rid of him, and that should be the end of it."

She took a drink and swallowed hard. "I'm not so sure. He said he knew something was fishy and he'd get to the bottom of it."

"Thus the appointment with me, right?"

"Maybe."

"April, what do you think he's after? Money?"

She shook her head. "Me. He came back here thinking I'd still be waiting for him, but when he found out I wasn't available, that made the prize all the more desirable. Stan is like a child. He wants all his toys around him, even though he doesn't play with them. As soon as someone takes one of the toys he's neglected, he immediately wants it back. He must have the upper hand in everything.

"That's why he came here and to my parents' house, to show he knew my routine, my life. He could find me anywhere. Thank

God he doesn't know where I live, though. I moved there after we broke up."

"And he knew how to get to you too, by luring you down here that day, alone."

She nodded, ashamed to admit he'd almost sucked her in again. She looked up into Michael's bright, intelligent brown eyes. "I'm grateful you showed up and brought me to my senses."

He smiled. "Glad I could help." He waited, then asked, "So why do you think he wants you back after all this time?"

She shifted in her seat. The only answer she could come up with had a bite of its own. Would Michael resent it or shrug it off?

"He's become successful and is ready to reap the rewards of his hard work. To maintain his status, he wants a wife on his arm for business functions, parties, and backstage support."

Michael sat back and stared unbelievingly. "Ouch." He rubbed a hand across his chin. "So you're thinking you're already stuck with this deal between us, when a better one comes along?"

"No! Stan, better? Never. The basis of his offer may have been the same, but the difference was, he *assumed* I would go through with it and *assumed* it would make me happy to be with him, finally. At least with you, I have a business deal. I know what to expect."

Michael's face tightened while he let that sink in. "So you don't love him?"

"I loved what we once had, but I know we'll never have it again. We're both different now, and I could never go back to the way it was."

Michael appeared almost relieved and resumed eating. Odd, but she felt relieved too. She'd admitted out loud that she no longer considered Stan a part of her life, and to the one person it shouldn't even matter to, yet somehow it mattered to her.

Michael double-checked the prospectus he'd printed up for his meeting with Stan Tragar. He liked to have preliminary information on hand for new clients, to personalize his service. But he needed to check one more mutual fund online before he put the package together.

Just then, Shelley buzzed his phone. "Michael, there's a Stan Tragar here to see you." He detected an unusually chipper lilt to her voice.

"Thanks. Tell him I'll be with him in a few minutes."

He closed his Internet browser and glanced at his appointment pad—Stan Tragar, Kleinman-Drexo Distributors, Inc. The name of Stan's employer didn't mean anything to him, but according to Stan they were big-time.

He picked up his phone and rang Kenny Gellar's office. "Ken, does the name Kleinman-Drexo Distributors mean anything to you? They deal in medical supplies." Kenny never forgot a company name once he'd heard or read about it.

"Hmm. I recall a Kleinman Industries and a Drexo Distributors a few years back. Both were big names in the medical supply field. Maybe there was a merger? I can look it up if you'd like. Why, what's up? A hot prospect?"

"Nah, just a client coming in who works for them. I'm curious if the guy is all smoke and mirrors or legit."

"I'll do a quick run on the name and get back to you if I find anything."

"Thanks, buddy."

Michael quickly cleared his desk of anything not pertaining to Stan Tragar and went to his office door to invite him in.

What he saw was Shelley batting her eyelashes and giggling like a schoolgirl to a very-close-over-the-desk Stan Tragar. Shelley tossed her hair to one side in a flirtatious move out of character for the usually poised, professional receptionist.

He closed his door soundly, intentionally startling them apart, then smiled as he approached the suave Stan in his thousand-dollar suit. Something inside him turned sunny-side up, grateful that April had escaped this snake.

Michael offered his hand. "Stan, good to see you again. Shelley, if Mrs. Goode calls, find out what time she'll be done, and I'll go down to meet her." He couldn't resist adding that piece of personal drama for Stan's sake.

Shelley smiled and lowered her gaze when Stan thanked her.

Stan had the good sense not to appear ruffled, either by Michael's comment or by his nearly inappropriate behavior toward Shelley. Instead, he sauntered beside Michael as casual and confident as could be and followed him to his office.

"Thanks for seeing me on such short notice. Great office, by the way." He looked around as though sizing up the competition.

"It's my home away from home."

"Not bad, but I bet it doesn't hold a candle to your home with April."

So, he wanted to play mind games. He'd come to the right place. "You got that right. She's completely turned my life around." *If he only knew.*

"Well, you seem pretty well-adjusted now." He took a seat and made a show of inspecting Michael's desk. "What, no pictures of her on your desk? No wedding ring for you either?"

Michael sat behind his desk and tipped his head toward Stan. "No wonder you've done well in business—you're very observant. Truth is, I've been a bachelor for so long, it's hard to shed the outer shell. We haven't gotten around to a ring for me yet because I'm not particularly fond of jewelry."

"Just seems odd, since April didn't have a ring either."

Michael sat forward, his gaze firmly locked on Stan's. "I get the feeling you're trying to make a point, but I'm not altogether sure what. Care to enlighten me?"

With a limp shrug, Stan broke the stare. "Just an observation. I mean, if she were my wife, she'd have an impressive rock to show for it."

Michael didn't doubt that for a minute. Stan undoubtedly made a career out of "showing" things. "Well, lucky for me, she's *not* your wife. In fact, I'd like to thank you for that lapse in good judgment. And she, in fact, does have a magnificent ring as a symbol of our devotion to each other. I just have to remind her more often that it belongs on her finger and not on the bathroom vanity."

Michael flashed a smile for emphasis and let that sink in for a moment before hitting him with the ace in the hole.

"But . . ." He turned to the bookcase beside his desk and lifted the large manila envelope. "You asked about pictures. That I have."

If only April could've seen Stan's face at that moment when he pulled the wedding album out and turned the pages, slowly, one by one, his surprise etching hard lines into his disbelieving face.

By the time he reached the last photo, he appeared almost disinterested. He slid the album back into the envelope. "Very nice. She sure made a beautiful bride."

"She's brightened every day for me since we met." And *that* was the truth. "But enough about me and April. Tell me about yourself, Stan. What brings you back to Rhode Island?"

"Business, mostly. We've expanded our sales force over the last two years, and our goal is to have at least one rep in every state. Since I'm familiar with Rhode Island, I volunteered to scope out the competition's presence and see where we can make a dent."

"Good game plan. With all the teaching hospitals and state-of-the-art medical facilities here, I'm sure you have a lot of ground to cover, and a lot of prospects for your medical supplies."

"Absolutely. I love a challenge."

"Is that why you've been sniffing around April? Another challenge because she took you off her waiting list?"

Stan paused at the quick change of topic, but his face never flinched. "April and I have a long history. It's only natural to try to hook up with old friends."

"The Friday lunch was one thing, but showing up at her parents' house with wild accusations is another. I wasn't able to be there that night, and I don't appreciate you bothering my wife. Do I make myself clear?"

"Perfectly. No harm intended. Like I said, we have a history, and sometimes old habits die hard. My apologies."

"I appreciate that. Now, tell me what you'd like Gellar Investments to do for you."

Michael wanted to get on with business, the quicker to get Stan out of there. He sat back and listened attentively as Stan summarized the last five years of his career, how he'd advanced quickly and gotten the promotion of a lifetime because of his dedication.

Michael found it difficult to believe that quality existed in someone like Stan.

"Well, Stan, we seem to have a lot in common, not the least of which is our choice of the same woman for a wife. But that shouldn't stand in the way of business or my attention to my client's needs."

Michael brought out the prospectus, some brochures, some mutual bonds printouts, and summarized what he thought might be a wise investment plan for someone in Stan's position and stage of life.

On a business level, the two men were synchronized. Each respected the other for his financial acumen. But on a personal level, Michael had a hard time swallowing the window dressing around Stan Tragar, and he detected a knowing glare in Stan's eyes that cautioned him not to trust anything this man said.

"Well, Michael, I have to say you're very thorough. I like what I see, and this firm's reputation precedes itself. In fact, I'm willing to take a recommendation back to the home office for the executive staff. With my seal of approval, you could see a lot of new activity."

"I appreciate that, Stan. You have my card—give me a call if you have any questions once you look over everything."

They shook hands after Stan rose and scooped up the folder Michael had prepared for him. "You'll be hearing from me soon," Stan promised. Or was it a warning? "Give my best to April."

After he left, Michael returned the wedding album to its place of honor on his shelf. Who'd've thunk a week ago that this anonymous little joke would affect so many people in so many different ways?

Michael turned to his computer and logged into his organizer to make an entry in his client profiles. After creating "Stan Tragar" and typing in the usual personal data to identify him, he jotted in the comments box: *balloon*. His code for *inflated; easily deflated*.

His phone buzzed, and he shouldered the receiver as he closed his organizer.

"Michael, I found Kleinman-Drexo Distributors. It *was* a merger between those two companies. I really had to dig to find anything that wasn't company promo. Looks like it's a strong company, plenty of money backing, but it seems top-heavy. Eighty percent of management is under age thirty-five and earning over $100K."

"So if the young blood don't seek out greener pastures, they'll be digging in for the long haul, looking for incentives, bonuses, and such."

"You got it."

Without a doubt, this client had to be handled carefully, both with his investments and his pursuit of one April Vaillancourt. The last thing he wanted to see was April retrace her steps, go back to Stan, and have him come up short as a good provider.

More to the point, the last thing he wanted was April out of his sight. Maybe he should take a quick run downstairs to make sure Stan didn't get sidetracked on his way out.

As soon as he opened his office door, he confirmed his suspicions. He'd gotten sidetracked all right, but right there at the reception desk. Taking up where he'd left off, Stan perched on the edge of Shelley's desk, leaning in close, talking in a low voice. Shelley blushed and fingered her hair, waiting on every word out of Stan's mouth.

A sudden realization hit Michael like a slab of fresh meat. *Not so long ago, that was me.* Ladies' man. Smooth talker. Do anything, say anything. He didn't like the mirror image. In fact, he retreated to his office to rethink what his own scheming had done to the man he once knew.

Michael looked at the clock, again. Only four. He wondered if April would pull another late night or if he could talk her into dinner. He knew she had to stay focused on her project, but with her only a few floors down, there was little else he could concentrate on, especially after his meeting with Stan Tragar.

A sharp rap on his door barely preceded Howard Gellar's abrupt entrance. "Michael, I'm on my way to meet Ben Aceto at the airport." Michael nodded, not surprised that Gellar would make the trek to Warwick himself for his longtime friend and number one client. "We'll be going out to dinner. Before I drop him off at his hotel, I thought we could swing by your place for a drink. I'd like him to get comfortable with you, see you in your domestic setting, meet the wife. Ben likes to do business with the whole person, not just the businessman."

Michael's pulse raced. *Meet the wife? Uh-oh.* "Gee, Howard, I think April's working late. Maybe some other time?"

The old man's face hardened. "Nonsense. By the time we have dinner and talk business, it'll be late enough for her to be home. Just give her a call to let her know we won't take up much time. One drink. Since you'll soon be handling his account, I want Ben to see how you make the best choices in both business and your personal life."

Michael heard the implication loud and clear. If he wanted that promotion, he had to follow the rules. Howard Gellar wanted to show off his handpicked successor like a proud father.

Nodding, Michael forced a smile. "I'm sure she'll be thrilled."

As soon as the old man left, Michael grabbed for the phone. "Tim? Michael Goode. I need to speak with April."

"Hey, Mike. Uh, she's not here."

"Not there?" A moment of panic rushed over him. Had Stan wormed his way back to her and lured her away? "Did she go home already?"

"No, she brought some proofs to our printer. She should be back shortly. What's up? Everything okay?"

Somewhat relieved, Michael raked a hand through his hair, pacing behind his desk. "Yeah . . . no. I have a problem, and I need her right away."

"Oh." Tim's concerned, one-word answer didn't sound very sincere.

"Listen, do me a favor. As soon as she gets back, tell her Gellar is bringing an important client to my house for a drink and to meet my wife. I need her there."

"Wife? You lost me. Why do you need April?"

A tiny alarm went off in Michael's head. "Didn't she tell you? Never mind, I don't have time to explain. I'm on my way home now. Have her call me right away." Michael rattled off his cell phone number, then hung up before Tim pressured him for any more details.

Even though he knew April was going to kill him, at least he could look forward to an evening with her.

"Whhhhat?" Twenty minutes later, April stood aghast as Tim explained the strange phone call from Michael Goode.

"He said he needed you there. What's going on, and what did he mean about the wife thing? I didn't think he was married, especially after that display in the elevator this morning. Are you the other woman, April?"

She waved her hand to banish the thought. "Don't be ridiculous. It's a long st—"

Tim caught her left hand as she sluiced it through the air and gazed down at the ring on her finger. "What the . . ."

She jerked her hand back and sidestepped to her computer. "It's not what you think. I can't explain right now."

"That's what he said."

"Tim, I promise I'll fill you in tomorrow. Right now just let me finish saving all these files and get out of here. I'll be in early tomorrow, I promise."

With some quick clicks, she backed up her day's work, then shoved all the art sheets and printouts into a folder. As she shut down her system, she picked up the phone and carefully dialed the number Tim had given her.

"Michael? What is going on? What am I supposed to do?"

"I'm sorry, April. I had no idea about this. Gellar just sprung this client meeting on me at the last minute. Can you get to my house right away?"

"Where do you live?" Tim cast her a strange look as she jotted down directions. "Okay, I'll be there as soon as I go home to change."

"There isn't time, April. Just come as you are."

"Michael, I have jeans on. I'm a mess. Let me at least freshen up my makeup."

"Okay, but I'm sure you look great. I'm just leaving the supermarket now. I picked up a few things to serve. I'll be home in ten minutes. Get there as soon as you can. And don't forget to wear the ring."

She twirled the gold and diamond band around her finger and swallowed a lump. "I have it on now." She ignored Tim's whistle.

Michael lowered his voice. "Good."

In the silence that followed, she wondered if she'd lost his cell phone connection, but then Michael murmured, "April?"

"Yes?"

"I'm glad this came up. Since the party, I've been dying to spend more time with you."

April bit her lip. How could she answer that? She'd felt the same way and had only managed to get through it by submerging herself in her work. Whenever someone came to the door, she'd look up with anticipation, hoping to see his face. When the phone rang, she listened for that smooth, deep voice to speak her name. Every moment had felt like ten, and if she had to sprout wings now to get to his side, well, she'd find a way.

But she couldn't think about any of that. She had to concentrate on being his wife, his temporary wife. They had no future as a couple.

With a catch in her voice she told him, "I'm on my way."

Chapter Eleven

April pulled up to the luxury condo village and sank back against her seat. Surprised at her surprise that he lived in such an upscale place, she shook her head, wondering what she was doing there. A wave of embarrassment flooded her memory as she thought of Michael's sleek black Vette parked in front of her nondescript apartment building two nights ago. Now here she was in her rusting pile of metal with the balding tires in front of his minicastle.

Her stomach knotted, and acid burned in her throat. This was crazy. How could she pull off pretending to live in such a place? She should've known better and told Michael she couldn't do it. In fact, she could still turn around and leave before she made a fool of herself, or him.

She shoved the key back into the ignition just as the front door opened and Michael flashed his million-dollar smile. He waved, looking casual in tan Dockers and a navy blue polo shirt. The acid retreated and was replaced by a sweet desire to kiss the man who now approached her with genuine appreciation in his brown eyes.

Removing the key from the steering column once again, she eased out of the car and into his welcoming embrace.

"You had me worried. I thought maybe you got lost."

"No, ran into traffic coming out of the city, and then I had to iron my blouse—"

"Never mind." He ushered her into the house. "You're here now, you look terrific, and that's all that matters." He elbowed the door shut, then whirled her into his arms again and hungrily kissed

124

her freshly glossed lips. "Mmm," he murmured, "I thought all day about doing that."

He kissed her again, more slowly this time, leaning in closer.

She giggled, removing her mouth from his. "I spent five minutes getting my lipstick on perfectly, and you've managed to ruin it in ten seconds."

"And what fun it was." He gave her another quick kiss, then released his bear hold. Looking down, he fingered the long black print skirt she wore. "Hiding your legs again, I see."

She tugged back the skirt. "My entertainment wardrobe is quite limited."

"Come on, you need to take a quick tour of *our* home so you'll know where things are."

Like a man possessed, Michael gave a whirlwind tour of his two-story condo, barely poking his head into each room.

Until they came to his bedroom. He stepped in, then stood back to let her survey the space.

Like Michael, it was sleek and masculine in an overpowering sort of way. The bed was king-size, naturally, with a plain dark gray coverlet and five huge pillows against the black metal headboard. Above the bed a large white ceiling fan spun lazily, its blades casting muted shadows from the center light. The few pieces of furniture—a chair, a small desk, end tables—all carried the gray and black theme to match the bed. The large window and sliding balcony door sported simple vertical blinds in a slate gray tone. In contrast to all the dark colors, the walls were off-white and free of decoration.

With the simplistic style of the room, she could just picture Michael's magnificence as the focal point in that big bed. Tall, lean, darkly handsome, he would be a perfect complement to the décor.

"Do you like?"

She dragged her eyes from the bed. "Like what?"

"My bedroom. They say a bedroom says a lot about a person."

"Really. Is that what you are? Black, white, and gray?"

Michael bunched his eyebrows, looking around at his room with a new clarity. He turned back to April. "No, I'm not. It never occurred to me those colors would indicate that. No, I'm not that at all."

The concern in his voice bordered on panic. He'd given off the wrong impression, and he obviously didn't want her to think of him in that way.

"Relax, Michael. It's just a bedroom with a masculine color scheme. Don't take it so seriously. It's a nice room. It's very you. I like it."

He let out a heavy breath. "Good."

Then her face turned serious. "So how did your meeting with Stan go?"

With the sudden confusion over Gellar's visit, he'd almost forgotten the eye-opening meeting with her ex-fiancé. If it were up to him, he'd forget it altogether and not let it come between them this evening. He'd stall for time and search for a way to ease her concern.

"Let's go downstairs, I have to finish some stuff in the kitchen. We can talk down there."

Michael opened the refrigerator door. But why? He couldn't remember what he'd gone in for. Closing the door, he stared at the handle. Oh, yeah, cheese. He opened the door again and grabbed the block of cheese he'd just bought.

"Can I do something?"

April's sweet voice barely broke through the fog in his brain. What was wrong with him? All week long people had been asking him if he was okay, as though his mind had strayed elsewhere.

And it had. To April. He'd found himself staring out windows, missing pieces of conversations, not hearing his phone until Shelley came in to see why he hadn't picked up. And when Howard had informed him of his plans to stop by, Michael nearly kissed his feet for giving him the perfect excuse to get April to his house.

He pointed to the ice maker and handed her a chrome ice bucket. "Could you get some ice?"

She smiled, apparently glad to be occupied. But he was definitely preoccupied. No woman—and he'd certainly had his share—had ever done this to him before. Was this why so many of his dates had called and nagged him for days afterward? Were they preoccupied too? Did they have this feeling of being lost without the person you I—

Michael dropped the cheese slicer on the counter, suddenly aware of where his thoughts had detoured. Love? Was this love? Was it possible to fall in love in such a short time? Was it even possible for *him* to fall in love?

He turned his head to watch April as she shook the bucket to disperse the cubes. A warmth flowed through his veins when she looked up and smiled. That smile had taken up permanent residence in his head since the first time he's seen it in the wedding album. Unlike in the photo, her smile now was for him and only him. He smiled back and vowed to do everything he could to earn that smile every day.

April carried the ice bucket to the small dry sink Michael had set up as his bar. She wondered why he was reluctant to talk about his meeting with Stan. Had Stan pressured him? Had he found out their secret?

It didn't seem likely, or he wouldn't have continued with this charade in front of Mr. Gellar tonight. Still, his awkward silence and quick glances unnerved her enough to make her guess that something was wrong.

If someone had told her a week ago that she'd be head over heels for a man who had everything any woman could possibly want, she would've scoffed at the thought.

Even more bizarre, he was the man she'd chosen as her April Fool's groom, who in turn had asked her to pose as his sometimes bride. Now that they were about to entertain in "their" home and go on a weekend cruise with his boss, she wondered how long she'd be able to keep her feelings in check. Falling for someone was hard enough, but the fall when he dropped you out of his life hurt even worse. Experience had taught her a hard lesson.

The doorbell rang, and she turned to him in panic. Michael flashed a reassuring smile after he put the last of the crackers on the cheese tray.

"Don't worry, you'll be fine."

She followed him to the front door and gathered her strength in the background as he greeted his guests. Howard Gellar wasted no time stepping forward with a fatherly hug.

"April! So nice to see you again. I'd like you to meet Ben Aceto, Gellar Investment's number one client. Ben, meet the woman who stopped Michael in his tracks."

April shook hands with the distinguished man with graying temples. His expensive suit and Italian leather shoes left no doubt he had money, but he also had a kind, friendly face that put her at ease immediately.

"A pleasure to meet you, April. You cost me a dinner tonight."

April's heart stopped. "I beg your pardon?"

Ben and Howard laughed together. Howard slapped Ben on the back. "Years ago he bet me that Michael would never settle down. Tonight he had to pay up."

Michael had come to her side and now eased his arm around her shoulders. "See that, hon? By marrying me, you made *two* men happy."

"Make that three," Ben added. "I gladly paid the tab to see someone tie you down, Michael."

They all laughed heartily.

Ben inclined his head. "But I need to ask you a favor, April."

She raised her eyebrows, wondering what this person she'd just met could possibly ask of her. "Sure."

"Because of Howard's choice of restaurants, my stomach is kicking up a fuss. Would you have some antacid?"

April almost blurted out "of course" until she remembered she wasn't in her own house. Antacid? Did Michael have any? Where would it be?

Obviously attuned to her dilemma, Michael came to the rescue. "I think I left it in the bathroom cabinet, honey. Check near the mouthwash." She turned to go, hoping she headed in the right direction, when Michael called out, "I'll get everyone set up with drinks. Want your usual, darling?"

Groaning to herself, she nodded. Her usual. Who knew what she'd come back to?

But to her surprise, a diet cola awaited her when she returned. He'd remembered from the party that she preferred soft drinks to hard liquor.

The next twenty minutes sped by as the men talked about stock options and market indicators. Howard and Ben had discreetly taken the green floral armchairs on opposite sides of the seating area, leaving the big sofa to April and Michael. He wasted no time cozying up to her after dispensing drinks.

The weight of his shoulder against hers soon sent heat coursing through her. Everything about Michael—his physique, good looks, and magnetism—distracted her every thought. If she was to get through this night, she had to forget the attraction and think about acting like a wife.

April followed the thread of the conversation with interest, nodding when a good point had everyone agreeing and frowning when opinions differed. She mentioned some new stocks she'd read about, and Howard seemed more than eager to voice his professional opinion.

When she asked Ben about his business' outlook for the remainder of the year, he went off on a litany of internal projects aimed at securing new customers. While listening intently, April greedily munched on cracker after cracker heaped with cheese chunks, since she'd missed dinner altogether.

"Well, our biggest jump in the new client market has been a direct result of our enviable Web site, and we have April to thank for that." Howard Gellar raised his drink in April's direction.

"April? You did the Web site?" Ben Aceto asked.

Choking down a bit of cracker, she shook her head. "No, not by myself. The company I work for produced and manages it."

Again, Howard hurried to sing her praises. "She's too modest. I know for a fact that she had a hand in every part of the project."

Ben nodded with interest. "Well, we'll have to get together on that subject real soon. Our Web site needs some serious revamping, and our current Web group just hasn't come up with anything powerful enough. If Howard is sold on you, that's enough to sell me."

"Web Works had it all over the competition when they made

their presentation," Howard asserted. "Lucky for Michael they did! I assume that's how you two met, right, Michael?"

Michael took a swallow of his drink, using the pause for effect. "Yes, that's right. We had a number of meetings to go over goals and expectations. April made it clear that this project was close to her heart, and that's what won her mine. When the final product ended up on my desk, I knew it would be a marriage made in heaven." He sent her a knowing glance.

"I have to admit," Howard chuckled, "you kept the romance a pretty good secret." He nodded to Ben. "He took off for an extended weekend trip, and the next thing we know, he's married!"

Michael laughed, sliding his arm around April and pulling her close. "Yes, well, before I knew it, she had me so besotted, I was begging her to be my wife." He gently shook her shoulders. "Isn't that right, honey?"

April forced a smile while wondering if anyone would notice a kick to his shins. She decided a verbal one was just as good.

"Michael, you're such a romantic. Actually"—she turned to their guests—"it was a mutual compulsion. I couldn't think of anyone I wanted more for a husband. He was picture-perfect."

Michael shot her an amused look that said, "Nice save," then leaned over and planted a kiss on her cheek. Turning to the men, he said, "See what I mean? How could I resist that?"

Howard laughed, then grunted as he got up from the chair. "Well, I think we've bothered you two long enough. I'm sure you have better things to do than entertain a couple of old fogies."

Ben rose. "Speak for yourself, old-timer. I'm not the one staring down the throat of retirement."

"Hey, I'm retiring while I'm still young enough to chase *my* bride around the house a few times. Now, let's get out of here so Michael can do the same."

The men said their good-byes and left the house with Howard's suggestion thick in the air. Michael clicked the door shut, turned a mischievous face to April, and waggled his dark brown eyebrows.

"You heard the boss. How much of a head start do you want?" Michael inched closer, reaching for her arm as she backed up a step.

"It's not funny, Michael. You don't know how hard that was, pretending."

He tugged her up against his chest. "I wasn't pretending."

She snapped her head back. "We're *both* pretending. There *is* no marriage. There *was* no wedding."

He relished the feel of her chest against him. Despite her tightly enunciated words, she didn't back away. She stood her ground, her way of asserting the nothing between them.

But, oh, was she wrong there. He'd seen her face when he kissed her cheek, felt her tremble when he touched her. He knew when a woman felt as attracted to him as he was to her.

But never had he seen one resist it so much. Was he losing his touch, or was April that one special person his father had warned him would turn his life around?

"So what's wrong with a little pretense? Didn't you ever play make-believe when you were a kid, as though you were living it for real? There's nothing wrong with a little fantasy. It's healthy."

"This isn't the same thing. We're pretending to be something we're not, and it affects other people's lives. Have you any idea how disappointed Howard would be if he found out? He was showing you off tonight like a proud father bragging about a son."

Michael knew she was right, and the thought of deceiving Howard was the one thing he regretted most about this whole crazy scheme. But he'd already set the machinery in motion—he was on his way to winning the promotion—and he couldn't very well stop it now. Even if he could, did he want to stop? This short time with April was the best he'd ever spent with a woman.

Almost made him think twice about bachelorhood.

Leaning forward, he kissed her on the nose. "I know you're right, but I also know that I haven't had to pretend very hard. I've enjoyed every minute with you, April, and apparently that was obvious to Howard, or he would've seen right through it the first day he met you. He reads human beings for a living."

"That's exactly why I'm so afraid of this cruise. One of us is bound to slip up and do something unmarried-like. Probably me."

"Well, then"—he snuggled a bit closer, rubbing his nose

against hers—"maybe we should spend all our time in our cabin, out of harm's way."

She smacked a hard fist against his chest. "That's not in the 'marriage' contract. And in case you've forgotten, you still haven't told me about your meeting with Stan."

Like a glass of water thrown in his face, the reminder of the irksome ex-boyfriend cooled his mood. He at least owed her an explanation and, if he could manage it, some assurance.

"Come on, let's sit down." They returned to the sofa, but this time she made sure she sat at arm's length. He wanted her close to him again, but as she pointed out, his make-believe and real life were getting mixed up in his jumbled brain.

"I won't lie to you and say it was strictly a business meeting, even though we did talk a lot about business. He actually does have money to invest and apparently has done well for himself." He stopped there. No need to go overboard with a glowing resume on Stan.

"But you were right about his suspicions. He made no secret that he thought our marriage was questionable. He's perceptive, if nothing else."

April closed her eyes and put her head in her hands. "I knew it. I knew this whole thing would blow up in our faces. He's going to ruin it, Michael. I know what he's like. When he has his mind set on something, it's a one-way ticket forward."

"Nothing has blown up, April. It's all under control. I'll handle it."

"You can't handle everything, Michael. I'm involved in this lie—all these lies—too. And they keep piling up. First I lied to you, then your receptionist, then Mr. Gellar, Stan, my parents, your client. Who's next? I can't keep all these lies straight! The only one who knows the truth is Kenny Gellar."

"What about Tim, your boss?"

She shook her head. "Oh, God, that's another one—well, not actually a lie." Then she managed a smile. "You should've seen his face when he saw the ring before I left today and I had no time to explain."

"He didn't notice it until today? You've had it on all week, haven't you?"

"Yes, but Tim is such a computer geek, when he works, he focuses on nothing except his screen. I've been just as bad this week, barely leaving my desk, so the extent of our interaction over the last three days has been 'good morning' and 'see you tomorrow.'"

Michael edged closer on the sofa. "Don't worry. I've got Stan under control. We came to an understanding that business and personal are separate. I'll do my best to advise him wisely as long as he keeps his nose clean."

She opened her mouth with a gasp. "Did you threaten him?"

"Threaten? Me? Of course not. I just enlightened him on some basic facts. He had you, he lost you, he blew it. Buh-bye."

She squinted at him. "Hmm, I'm very aware of how you 'enlighten' people. In fact, I seem to recall another meeting in your office less than a week ago—"

"Okay, okay, so you know I play to win." He put his hand to her face. "But look how far we've come. A week ago we didn't even know each other."

"I'm beginning to wonder if those were the good old days."

He stroked her cheek and saw that sparkle he loved in her eyes. "There's the April I know. Keep that flame glowing, and we'll breeze right through this deal."

"Or burn ourselves out trying."

With a laugh, he removed his hand from her face and took her hand instead. "If it'll make you feel any better, I think Stan is already distracted."

"Distracted? What do you mean?"

"He had a serious flirtation going on with Shelley."

"What? Oh, no! What if he shares his suspicions with her? What if she believes him?"

"Calm down. It won't happen. First of all Shelley firmly believes we're married. She saw the album, she's seen us together, and remember, she thinks you're pregnant."

"Oh, God, I forgot that."

"Second, Shelley is the queen of gossip. When she gets a snippet of it, to her it's gospel. I'm sure she's already shared this with any number of office 'confidantes.' She'd have to save face by sticking to her guns."

With another sigh followed by a stifled yawn, she murmured, "I don't know how much more of this mess I can take." Pulling away, she rose and strode to the kitchen to retrieve her purse.

"Are you leaving?"

"Yes. My brain needs some rest, and I have to get to work early tomorrow."

"Sure I can't convince you stay any longer?"

Balefully shaking her head when she returned, she put a hand out to brush him aside, but he caught it up in his own and enveloped her in his arms. She struggled only for a second, then molded her body to his as he brought his mouth down to meet hers.

"Thank you for coming," he murmured.

She licked her lips. "You're welcome."

"I mean that sincerely. I don't know what I would've told Howard if you hadn't showed. And you were great. I mean, sitting through that boring business talk was pretty heroic."

"I enjoyed it, actually. It's fun peeking into the mind of a genius."

"You can peek into my mind anytime."

"I meant Howard."

With a hearty laugh, Michael turned and led her to the front door. "Come on, I'll walk you to your car."

Chapter Twelve

April barely had her eyes open the next morning when she stepped off the elevator and into the crowded office of Web Works. Not that two people were a crowd, but when one of them was Michael Goode, the King of Charm, and the other was Tim Houghton, whose eyes were as big as the lid on her coffee cup, it left little room for a tired, frazzled April.

"April, Mike just filled me in on the outrageous scam you two have going." Tim looked as though he'd just been handed the scoop of the century. He really needed to get away from his computer more.

She managed to avoid Michael's look for only a moment. Drawn to his captivating smile and smoldering dark eyes, she feared her desire for him this morning exceeded her attraction last night.

But the fact remained that she was being paid for this role, more or less, and if she allowed this attraction to become more, what did that say about her character? In this manufactured relationship she had no one to blame but herself for feeling belittled. If she hadn't made that wedding album, and if someone hadn't recognized Michael, none of this would've happened.

She might never have met Michael either.

She might've missed his smile, his laugh, his sharp comebacks. She wouldn't have experienced the most delicious kisses and heated stares. One short week of all these milestones already added up to certain heartbreak. She knew her feelings for him ran much deeper than she allowed herself to admit, and she saw the inevitable charging toward her like a raging bull.

When this was over, when Michael got his promotion, she'd be left with a relationship that didn't exist. Once again, she'd be the woman left behind by a man moving forward.

At least this time, she knew in advance.

"It's not a scam, Tim. It's a . . ." She struggled for a word to describe a falsehood that had taken her for an unexpected ride on a runaway train. "It's Michael's way of securing a promotion and my way of making up to him for my irresponsible act."

Tim and Michael turned to each other as though trying to read each other's mind. "Geez, it sounds so cold and calculating coming from her. I think I liked your version better, Mike."

Michael nodded thoughtfully. "Yes, well, April is serious about her new tires."

Exasperated with their mocking humor, she dropped her handbag and briefcase near her desk and nudged Michael's foot off her chair as she placed her coffee out of hand-swinging range.

"Would you mind removing your bottom from my desk? I have work to do."

"See, Tim? Spoken like a true wife, already ordering me around."

The two men laughed, and April glared at Tim from behind narrowed eyelids. To Michael, she waved her hand as though swatting a fly from her desk.

"Aw, I just came in to say good morning and to apologize to Tim for being so abrupt on the phone yesterday. Between the two of us, we really put him through the wringer."

"I'm sure he'll get over it." She dropped heavily into her seat.

"Be nice, now. We can use another ally on our side, and Tim's quick thinking helped us get rid of Stan the other day."

Tim beamed at the camaraderie the two of them had apparently forged in her absence.

Michael slid off the desk and walked behind her chair. She sensed his hand on the back of the seat and wished he'd touch her, tell her that he wanted to be with her no matter what.

Instead, he made his way around to the front, clearing his throat. "Well, I'd better get upstairs. I have an early meeting with a client. Tim, good luck with that new account you're bidding on, and, April . . ." His heavy pause on her name sent shivers down her spine. His eyes burned into hers. "Thanks again for last night. You were terrific."

With a wink and a smile, he left the office. Though not completely. The fresh scent of his aftershave lingered around her desk. The air crackled with intensity. She could still hear his voice, mellow and suggestive. There wasn't a part of her that didn't ache for Michael Goode. Now, if she could only convince her body how wrong it was.

April stared straight ahead at her blank computer screen.

"It works much better if you turn it on," Tim suggested.

She pressed the power button and waited as the screen came alive with internal system checks. Too bad she didn't have that luxury—a routine to prevent and correct fatal errors. It might've stopped her the day she edited those photos or, better, the day she agreed to this scheme.

"Tim, do you think I'm crazy for going through with this?"

"April, how many years have I known you? I've seen you do a lot worse."

"Thanks for the vote of confidence."

"Come on, April. Mike's a great guy. How can you go wrong?"

"I already did. Howard Gellar doesn't deserve this kind of deceit. He's a really nice guy, and he has so much faith in Michael."

"Then I'd say that's Michael's problem, not yours."

"I'm just afraid the whole thing will blow up in his face. Gellar will find out, he won't promote Michael, or, worse, he'll fire him, Michael will hate me, and it'll be all my fault."

"Hate you? The guy is nuts about you!"

"It's an act, Tim. He's playing the part of a smitten newlywed."

"Really? He doesn't have to pretend around me. I'm not the one he has to convince, and from what I've seen, the smitten part is real. The way he looks at you, I'd say you could get a whole lot more than a set of tires."

She shook her head sadly. Material things.

"I don't want anything more," she mumbled.

Tim cautiously stepped to the front of her desk and stared while a little choking sound escaped his open mouth.

"You're in love with him! That's what's bothering you, isn't it?"

April buried her face in her hands and shuddered as a deep intake of breath went through her whole body. "I don't know what love is, Tim, but this is the closest I've ever come to feeling it."

"Then why so glum? You should be happy."

She lowered her hands. "Happy? Happy that when this is all over he'll walk away, and I'll never see him again? Happy that I've lost another chunk of my heart?"

Tim pushed his face to within inches of hers until she saw her reflection in his glasses.

"Then it's up to you to tell him how you feel."

"Not a chance."

"Stubborn to the end, huh? I hope those new tires keep you warm at night."

Late that afternoon, April looked up to see Michael in the doorway. She couldn't stop the smile that pulled at her lips to match his. After staring at HTML code and graphics all day, she found him to be more than a welcome sight, smiling and glowing in his still-starched white shirt and royal blue tie. Even with his five o'clock shadow making an early appearance, he looked as fresh as he had that morning.

"How's the new project going?"

She stretched back in her chair and rolled her shoulders. "I had a breakthrough day. All the little annoying pieces started falling into place. A few more days of polishing, tying up loose ends, then testing."

"Great, then maybe you'll be ready for a little R and R tomorrow night?"

"Now what?"

"Tomorrow night is Company Night at McCoy Stadium, our yearly PawSox outing. Ever go to the Pawtucket Red Sox games?"

"Not for years."

"So, will you join me? The whole office will be there. It would be the perfect place for us to be seen together."

Just then Tim returned from his trek to the post office.

" 'Seen together'? Another planned sighting of the Goode new-lyweds?"

"Help me out here, Tim. Gellar's annual night at McCoy. Tell her what a great time we'll have at the PawSox game."

"Dude, I love the PawSox! You should go, April. Their games are always awesome."

Michael fanned a stack of tickets in front of him. "Why don't you come too, Tim? I have plenty to go around."

"Yeah? Nah, I'd feel out of place. I don't work there or anything. . . . Yeah?"

Michael laughed. "Come. You can sit with us. Plus, you know the people from marketing, and you know Shelley, the recep-tionist."

To April's amazement, Tim actually blushed at the mention of Shelley's name. Did Tim have a crush on her? How had she missed that? It sure explained his frequent trips upstairs to "drop off" reports. Maybe a little test would prove her theory.

"So Shelley is going too?" she asked Michael.

"She always does. Her chance to let down that professional guard and cut loose."

Tim's blush deepened, and he turned away to fumble with some folders on his desk. April nearly choked with the laugh she had to stifle.

"Well, if you have plenty of tickets, I guess I'll take one," he finally relented.

"Here ya go, my friend. You can have two if you want to bring a date."

Tim quickly turned back to his desk, mumbling under his breath, "No, just one. One's enough. Thanks."

"You're welcome to drive in with us."

"Nah, I'll take my own car, you know, in case I want to leave early or something . . . or if you guys do . . . oh, you know what I mean."

Yes, April knew. A player had to leave his options open, after all. Couldn't be weighed down by an old married couple.

April smiled at Michael. "I think I'm actually looking forward to this game now."

"That makes three of us, then."

April tried on at least five sweaters while getting ready for her date with Michael Friday night. Correction. Not a date. A date had nothing to do with two people pretending they were married. A date usually involved two people playing the mating game, dancing to their emotions, elevating a relationship to the next level.

This was nothing of the sort. The only reason Michael and April were together resulted from an arrangement that had nothing to do with mating, dancing, or a relationship. She probably should write that down and repeat the mantra at least twice a day.

Tonight, at least, her job would be easier. No fancy dress, no small talk over drinks, no cautious table manners. Tonight, she'd be a part of a crowd, an audience filled with all kinds of people, single, married, dating, friends. She could be herself without worrying what she said to whom.

She finally decided on the right sweater just as Michael arrived. It was bulky enough to keep her warm in the early-spring air but tight enough to flatter her. No reason not to look as good as possible.

"Hi," he breathed softly when she opened the door. "Ready for a ball game?"

She laughed at *his* sweater. "Are you sure *you're* ready? Do you think white is such a wise color when we'll be eating hot dogs with ketchup and pretzels with mustard?"

He cocked his chin up with confidence. "I'm a very neat eater." He then tweaked her nose gently. "But just in case, I have a jacket in the car."

She laughed and grabbed her own jacket, then followed him down the stairs to his sleek black Vette. Good thing Tim had declined a ride—where would he sit? She quickly erased a vision of her sitting in Michael's lap.

Since April lived in Pawtucket, it didn't take them long to get to the ballpark, and they were early enough that the traffic didn't hold them up. They took their time entering the stadium, went straight to the concession stands, and each came away with a tray full of junk food to be balanced on their laps once they found their seats.

Quick to bite into her hot dog, April almost forgot they'd be meeting other people and putting up a front. She chewed aggressively while watching from her first-baseline seat as the players practiced on the field. Engrossed with her food and the sights, she nearly jumped when Tim came up next to her.

"Hey, guys."

"Yo, Tim, glad you could make it." Michael and Tim tipped manly nods to each other.

After a hard swallow of her mouthful, April offered her tray of bounty. "Want anything?"

"Nah, I already had a bunch. I got here early." Tim looked around, appearing uncomfortable in the surroundings. Without a doubt, he hung around computers too much.

With a mental shake, April cautioned herself not to judge. After all, that's what her family and friends said about her, and mostly it was true. But compared to Tim, she was a downright party animal.

"You guys are the only ones I see here from Gellar. Are you sure they're coming?"

"Relax, Tim, the others will trickle in. A lot of the office staff was still there when I left."

"Oh, so I guess Shelley was still at the reception desk?"

He couldn't be more transparent if he'd been the Invisible Man! But April promised herself not to tease the wallflower. He deserved to dream too. She of all people should be the last to tease anyone about pining after someone else. She'd done her share over the years. And Tim could give as well as he could take if the situation were reversed.

Michael and April continued to eat while the three of them exchanged small talk about work, the players, the cool air. A few more people from Gellar Investments arrived and took seats in front of and behind them. Tim continued to fidget, looking back, craning his neck until the anxiety got the best of him.

With a quick jerk, he stood. "I'm going to get a soda. Anybody want anything?"

Michael waved a hand. April shook her head. "You could dump this trash if you wouldn't mind."

He took their trays and shot out of the row. As soon as he'd left, April snickered under her breath.

"What's so funny?" Michael asked.

"Tim. He's acting like a teenager waiting for the pretty girl to walk by him in the cafeteria."

He frowned and shook his head. "You lost me."

"Don't you get it? The only reason he came here tonight was because you said Shelley was coming. I'm surprised he hasn't given himself whiplash from turning his head around so much."

Michael's eyes widened with enlightenment. "No kidding . . . he likes Shelley? You know, now that you mention it, he does hand-deliver a lot of the Web and marketing reports that could easily be faxed or e-mailed."

"Duh."

"Maybe I'll put in a good word for him—"

"Don't you dare. Let Tim work on this in his own good time, at his own speed."

"You're right. There's nothing worse . . ."

Michael's sentence trailed off as his gaze focused on something at the end of the row behind April. "What?" She turned to follow his now-gaping stare and saw Shelley walking in with none other than Stan Tragar. The snake in the grass.

"Oh, no."

"Oh, no."

The couple made their way to their seats, directly behind April, two rows up. Shelley gushed her greeting to April and Michael, while Stan's smug smile said it all. He'd wormed his way into a date to spite April and to keep an eye on her all at the same time. With or without a threat from Michael, Stan still had his suspicions, and April would be wise to steer clear of him.

He'd also unknowingly stuck a pin into Tim's bubble.

"Well," sneered Michael, "I should've seen that one coming."

She whispered back, "You did say they had some serious flirting going on. We shouldn't be all that surprised."

"No, but I think I overestimated Shelley's good sense." He

turned to greet another co-worker who'd come in behind him, then tipped his head back to April. "Do you know she actually chastised me the other day about my behavior toward women? After meeting you, she said I 'done good' this time, so you have her stamp of approval."

"Swell, approval from someone who takes to the likes of him." She jerked her thumb to the back rows.

He laughed. "In any case, she was right. I done good." He put his arm around her and rested his sweet-smelling head on hers.

"But this relationship was more an accident than a choice, an accident that turned into a troublesome plan."

He kissed her temple. "A very good plan, I might add."

She closed her eyes and for a moment allowed herself to believe he held her and kissed her because he wanted to, not because it was part of the act. The warmth she felt came as much from the closeness of his body as from the feelings he stirred within her. April found her heart rate picking up and her mind wandering to far-off places she once feared she'd never go: love, marriage, family.

Why couldn't she have met Michael Goode under different circumstances? Why couldn't they have a relationship based on love and trust instead of deceit and bargains?

Because that didn't appear to be her lot in life. She'd wasted too many years waiting for an absent love to return and for promises to be fulfilled. Stan had taught her a valuable lesson. Nothing is as it seems. Hopes and dreams can quickly evaporate into the thin air they are made of, once you open your eyes.

She opened her eyes then and looked down at her hand, securely held by Michael's. How soon before this dream ended?

A rustling sound beside her pulled her from her deep thoughts. Tim had returned, soda in hand, his face drawn. No doubt he'd seen Shelley.

"Looks like the Gellar population has arrived," he quipped none too happily.

April scanned the stands around her and saw that Connie and Howard Gellar had shown up with their daughter and granddaughter. Kenny Gellar and his wife were heading down the steps.

One by one, Stan schmoozed with each of them as Shelley proudly introduced him and clung to his side.

April wanted to throw up.

Instead, she patted Tim's arm. "Tim, on any other day you and I would be as out of place with this assemblage as polar bears in Hawaii. But we're at a ball game, which puts us all on a level field. Let's just enjoy the game. Monday we'll go back to our cave, where we're most comfortable."

The poor guy hunkered down in his seat and turned up his collar. April almost wished Michael hadn't given him the ticket.

Between innings, Howard Gellar made the rounds, greeting his employees and their families. Savvy to a fault, he knew the right thing to say to everyone, acknowledged the spouses by name, handed out hats and bags of peanuts to the kids. His gruff exterior took a backseat to his kind heart when it came to family.

Michael watched and learned. If he had any chance of moving up to the CEO position, following Howard's lead would serve him well.

Which brought to mind something April had said the other night. Deceiving Howard with this false marriage could backfire and ruin not only Michael's career, but also the strong bond he'd forged with Howard over the years. April's observation about Howard treating him like a son was right on the mark. His own father had taught him everything he needed to achieve success. But Howard had taught him how to make success work for you.

At the end of the fourth inning, Howard made his way over. "How are my two favorite newlyweds?" He pumped Michael's hand and bent to kiss April on the cheek. "Nothing like a spring night at a ball game to bring a family together, eh?" He nodded past April. "Hello, Tim, good to see you. Everyone having a good time?"

"Great, Howard," Michael said. "Always a fun night."

"The game's not bad either. They might actually squeak this one out for a win!" Howard's hearty laugh turned most heads in his direction. "Say, who's that fellow with Shelley?"

Michael hoped Howard didn't notice Tim sink deeper into his

seat or April clamp her mouth shut. "He's a prospective client I met with on Wednesday, Stan Tragar. Seems he and Shelley hit it off immediately."

"I got an uneasy feeling about him when I went over to talk. Surprised he can sit up straight with that big ego weighing him down."

April covered a smile with her hand, while Tim folded his arms across his chest.

"Don't worry, Shelley can take care of herself."

"Oh, I know that. She's the only other woman besides my wife who can tell me what to do. Not that I listen, but she's usually right. You just make sure you check him out thoroughly before committing to any long-term contract with us."

"I'm already on it, Howard."

"Good. Enjoy the game." He leaned close and lowered his voice for privacy. "I'll see you next weekend on the cruise, April."

As soon as Howard left, Tim sat up, eyes wide open with disbelief. April clamped down on his hand with a warning.

"You're going on a cruise?"

She gritted her teeth. "Quiet. We don't need the world to know."

Michael leaned across April and spoke softly. "Howard's yacht. He invited us for a long weekend to celebrate our marriage."

Tim's mood seemed to momentarily lighten. "First a wedding, now a honeymoon. How about that?" He jabbed April with his elbow. "What's next, a baby?"

When April's face tightened and she stared straight ahead, Michael offered an explanation. "Shelley already thinks a baby's on the way. You know, the quickie wedding, the teddy bear balloon, April's nervousness every time she's in the office. Not to mention your panicked call the other day when Stan showed up and you said that April had a problem."

Tim's chuckle started low, then rumbled and shook his shoulders. "Oh, this is priceless."

"Go ahead and have your fun," she warned. "While you two are having a good laugh at my expense, I'm sitting here freezing. Would one of you care to get me something hot to drink?"

"I'll go," Michael said. "I'll run back to the car and grab the blanket I meant to bring in too."

He rose and turned, then decided a little drama was in order for the sake of those around them. He bent down, took April's face in both hands, and kissed her fully and greedily.

Then, in a voice just a little too loud, he said, "That's to keep you warm until I get back." He heard Shelley's "aww" from two rows back and looked sideways to see Stan glaring straight at him.

He left the stands an inch taller than when he'd walked in.

April huddled in her seat, her jacket pulled tightly around her, her teeth chattering. The wind direction had changed, and the cool night air had now turned cold. She shivered, hoping Michael would hurry back with the blanket and hot drink.

But the cold worked its way through her, and she couldn't wait any longer. "Tim, I'll be right back. I have to go to the ladies' room."

She excused her way out of the row, then up the stairs. She searched for the signs pointing to the restrooms, and that's when she noticed Michael with his back to her, talking to a shapely brunet who seductively leaned into him.

Struck with an inexplicable blast of jealousy, April couldn't help but stare. He'd gone from loving husband to playboy bachelor in the blink of an eye. So much for role-playing. As her cold body warmed with welling anger, she forced herself to turn away and dash for the ladies' room.

Once inside the stall, hidden from prying eyes, she wiped at tears she shouldn't be shedding. There was nothing between them, no promise of faithfulness, and certainly no vows to uphold. Michael could do whatever he wanted with whomever. The ring on her finger meant nothing except that she'd done a foolish thing and was now paying for it.

Then she turned her anger on herself for letting her feelings go so far. She knew Michael's outward expressions were part of the act, especially that kiss back at the seats. She could only blame herself for holding out hope that he might be sincere.

But what about the times when they were alone? The kisses in the elevator, at his house, his close attention when they'd shopped for her dress? Was that for her benefit or his?

She dried her eyes and braced herself for the truth. He liked women. He charmed them, wooed them, and generally left them. Like Stan. Her taste in men hadn't changed after all.

When April finally left the restroom, she stole a glance in the direction she'd seen Michael, but he was gone, and so was the brunet. She let out a breath of relief, then turned and came face-to-face with Stan.

"Your husband should be more attentive. You never know who you might run into out here alone."

Chapter Thirteen

You ou mean, someone like you?"

"I mean someone who might think you're unattached."

April stiffened at Stan's insinuation. "And where's your lovely date?"

"Ooooh, sarcasm tinged with jealousy? I like that."

She started to walk away, but Stan held her arm. "Take your hand off me, and don't think for a minute I have any emotions left for you, the least of which would be jealousy."

He promptly released her arm. "Aw, April, why can't we be friends? I hold no animosity toward you, even though you ran off and got married after promising your love to me."

"That promise was *years* ago. All it got me was a lot of long, lonely nights and weekends."

"I know. I didn't realize what I had, and now I've lost it, but it's a hard lesson learned. I'll admit that at first it wasn't easy to see you two lovebirds together, but I like Michael, and I think he's good for you. I can see how much he means to you, and he's certainly affectionate. I hope it lasts long after the two of you are three."

She jerked her head up and was about to blast him with a bitter tirade when Tim came out of nowhere and stood by her side. "Ah, so Shelley spilled the beans, huh? See, April? I told you people would figure it out. You can only keep a baby a secret for so long."

Stan's face hardened, although April couldn't decide if it was from being interrupted or because he'd thought he had another dirty secret on April. Still, he continued in an even tone.

"A quickie, hush-hush wedding doesn't help, that's for sure. I must say, I wasn't quite convinced about the wedding at first, but this added twist answers why. You surprise me, April, getting yourself into that predicament."

She was about to step forward and slug Stan in his fancy belt buckle when Tim stepped between them.

"Your hot chocolate is getting cold back at your seat, and Michael's waiting with your blanket." Tim nudged her as if to say, go, this is your chance.

"I must have been a fool to ever think you were the right man for me." With a searing final glare, she turned to leave, but not before hearing Tim's parting words.

"Oh, and, Stan, I had a little talk with Shelley. She had no idea you strung April along for years."

Michael watched the stairs. What was taking April so long? Tim said she'd only gone to the ladies' room, but he'd been back for ten minutes now, and no sign of her. He'd noted that Stan was among the missing as well and that Shelley had looked none too happy after Tim exchanged a few words with her on his way out.

He shouldn't have stopped to talk to Brenda, but he hadn't seen her in two years, and she couldn't wait to tell him she was married. He came close to saying the same to her but stopped himself at the last minute.

No, he wasn't married. All this pretending was getting confusing. He had to remember where he was and whom he was talking to before saying the wrong thing.

But darn if he didn't feel married whenever he was around April. It went beyond pretense, something he couldn't explain except that it felt so good.

Finally, he saw her blond curls bouncing down the steps. She got to her seat quickly and without even a glance at him.

Odd. "Here, let's put this blanket over us."

He spread the wool across the two seats and tucked it around her to keep the cold out, then handed her the cup of chocolate. She wrapped both hands around the warm cup and sipped greedily but still said nothing.

"Are you okay? You were gone quite a long time."

Staring straight ahead, she agreed. "I could say the same about you."

"I know. I ran into an old friend. Had a tough time getting away from her."

"I bet."

He tilted his head to get a better look at her face, but she didn't return his gaze. If he didn't know better, he'd think she was angry. No, wait, not angry . . .

"Is that jealousy?"

She tugged the blanket tighter around her, ignoring his face in her face. "What are you talking about?"

A little bubble burst inside his chest, and Michael felt a warm sensation rush through his veins. He'd never thought that being on the receiving end of jealousy could be so invigorating.

"It is. You're jealous." The crowd jumped up and cheered a home run, but Michael could've cared less. He felt as though he'd just hit a grand slam. "I'm flattered. Truly. But if it makes you feel any better, Brenda and I hadn't seen each other in two years, and she was telling me about her recent marriage."

April stole a sideways glance, her face softening at the explanation. "Really?"

"Really. I'm all yours."

She reddened but smiled.

"Do you have any idea how beautiful you look right now? I could just eat you up!"

He quickly tugged the blanket over their heads and took her mouth in a teasing, hungry fashion with growling sound effects, much to her giggling delight. But as soon as his lips settled in for a kiss, he tossed the kidding aside and let his passion take over. He loved kissing April Vaillancourt, and he loved the way she kissed him back. The heck with the crowd around them yelling about some great play. He'd just slid into home.

When the game ended, they slowly filed out of the stadium while talking to the rest of the Gellar people. That's when he noticed that Shelley and Stan weren't among them.

"I saw them leave shortly after I got back from the men's room," Tim noted with a smile. "Neither of them looked too happy."

April snickered into her jacket.

Michael looked from one to the other. "I get the feeling I missed something."

April filled him in after they got into the car. Within minutes they'd reached April's house. He walked her up the stairs to her apartment, unwilling to let the night end so soon. But April had different ideas. She unlocked her door and turned to him.

"I guess I'll see you Monday."

"How about joining me on my run tomorrow?"

"Uh-uh. Too many things to do."

"Dinner tomorrow night?"

She shook her head. "I'm babysitting for a friend."

"Sunday, then?"

"I'm having dinner at my parents'."

He leaned closer and took a whiff of her intoxicating scent. He needed something to hold him over.

"Let me go with you."

"To my parents'? What for?"

"To meet them. I'd love to know the people who created you."

"That's ridiculous. There's no reason for you to go there and meet them."

He crooked his finger under her chin. "What if Stan shows up again, asking questions?"

Her frightened look told him she knew he was right, especially after tonight, when Stan's game plan had been undermined by Tim. Michael sent a telepathic high five to Tim. *Way to go, dude.*

April nipped at her bottom lip, thoughtful on how to answer.

"If I bring you, will you promise to agree that the pretending to be married was all your idea and that it was only to get rid of Stan? My mom still thinks we could get back together if I just gave him a chance."

"I promise to take full responsibility for any untruths, and I will charm your mother into forgetting all about Stan what's-his-name."

"Easy on the charm. We don't want her getting the wrong idea."

"What kind of wrong idea?"

"That there's anything between us."

"There's not? Then I need to convince *you* a little more."

He leaned into her until she backed to the door. He found her mouth in an instant and kissed it wide and full until her arms circled his neck and she moaned softly. His own groan rose to meet hers.

Reluctantly, he broke the kiss. With a touch to her cheek, he promised, "I'll call you."

She slept until noon on Sunday. Babysitting for her friend Michelle's kids Saturday night had completely wiped April out, but what were best friends for if she couldn't watch the kids on the couple's anniversary?

To her complete delight, she'd woken to Michael's phone call, his voice so familiar now, it played almost nonstop in her head. And she didn't have to hide her smile over the phone. Instead, she stretched languidly on the bed, the receiver cradled on her shoulder.

"So what time should I pick you up?"

"How about four? I try to get there early to help Mom with dinner, even though she has most of it done already."

Punctual as ever, Michael arrived at four. Helping himself to a little before-dinner treat, he kissed her in the doorway as they left her apartment. She remembered the last kiss they'd had in that same spot and couldn't forget the feelings it had evoked in her. Michael had left that night, but his kiss had lingered long after, through brushing her teeth, washing her face, and far into the night as she dreamed of a life with Michael that wasn't a lie.

But this kiss came from a softer, gentler Michael. One that didn't hurry, didn't demand. She enjoyed the feel of his lips, soft when they touched but firm in their purpose. And she enjoyed kissing him back, especially when he smiled at the end. That dimple weakened her knees every time.

They arrived at her parents' not long after. Michael rumbled his Corvette into the narrow driveway of the small Cape house nestled in a neighborhood of a dozen other Capes all the same but painted different colors.

"If my dad doesn't say much, don't worry—he's not much of a talker."

"And your mom?"

"She'll talk your ear off if you give her half a minute."

"They know I'm coming, right?"

"Yes, I called Mom yesterday. God forbid she shouldn't have enough food."

They went in the side door, through the breezeway that connected the house to the one-car garage. Her mother was taking out the dishes to set the table.

"Hi, Mom. This is Michael Goode, a friend from work."

Her mother wiped her hands on a towel and shook hands. "I'm so glad you could come, Michael. Friends of April are always welcome here. When she called to ask if you could come, it was without question."

"Thank you, Mrs. Vaillancourt, but I'm afraid I'm here on my insistence, not because April invited me. I told her I had to meet the two wonderful people who'd brought her into this world."

April rolled her eyes as her mother blushed. She actually blushed! The Michael Goode charm had done it again.

"Come on, Michael, I want you to meet Dad." They didn't have to look for long. On a Sunday afternoon, he didn't stray far from the TV.

"Dad, this is Michael Goode."

Her father stood and shook hands, sized up Michael in a few seconds with a quick nod, then sat back down to watch the Red Sox game.

"Think they'll do it again this year?" Michael gestured toward the screen.

"Without a doubt. We know nothing is impossible anymore."

With that, the two men bonded, and April breathed a sigh of relief. She returned to the kitchen to help her mother, assured she didn't have to "watch" Michael for now. Dad wouldn't talk about much else besides the game and the players.

"April, he's positively hunky!"

"Shh, Mom, he'll hear you."

She lowered her voice. "He looks like William Storrs on *The Wind and the Sea*."

"Mom, I'm not up on soap operas anymore, so I wouldn't know."

"And he's so charming. Oh, I like him better than Stan already."

"Me too, but to be honest, anyone is better than Stan."

She helped her mother finish setting the table, getting the vegetables ready, and popping some biscuits into the oven. By five, they all sat down, and the great moment of silence began. April knew that Michael and her dad had probably depleted the sports discussions. She also knew that her mother was itching to hear all about Michael. And April just wanted the meal to end so she didn't have to pretend anymore.

"So, Michael, what is it that you do?" A record for Mom— thirty seconds.

"I'm an investment analyst and consultant with Gellar Investments in Providence. We're one of the largest investment firms on the East Coast with clients all over the country."

April watched her Mom blink, having no clue what an investment analyst did. Her dad glanced at Michael above a forkful of food, impressed with the fancy job description.

"That sounds wonderful. Do you like it?"

"Very much. Every day brings something exciting to the table. I get to play with other people's money."

"Now, that sounds scary to me. I'd be afraid to have someone else's money."

Michael laughed. "It can be intimidating sometimes, if you allow yourself to think of it that way. I prefer to look at it like an Erector set. I take a little money at a time and build it up into something large and useful."

Once again, her mother stared blankly, baffled by the concept of building with money.

"Now, how did you two meet, again?" She looked from April to Michael as though she wanted an explanation from both.

April decided to keep it short. "At work."

But Michael couldn't resist embellishing the story, despite her earlier warnings. "April and Tim take care of our firm's Web site, so we sort of ran into each other one day. We've been inseparable ever since."

If she kicked him under the table, would he blab about that too?

"Oh, I don't understand much about Web sites or that Internet stuff. I know it's what April does, but the whole idea is beyond me. I'll stick to my sewing."

"Your sewing?" Michael asked with interest.

Her mother beamed, but April jumped in with her chance to brag. "Mom is amazing with a sewing machine. She does custom curtains. Something she started as a hobby when I was in grammar school, but it quickly turned into a small home business. She did all the curtains in here."

Michael looked around with an admiring eye. "Beautiful work, Mrs. Vaillancourt. Maybe I should have you do some for me. I seem to have a black, white, and gray identity problem in my house."

April was about to stomp on his foot for his reference to her comment about his décor, when the screech of racing tires out front distracted them all.

Her father got up, mumbling under his breath, "Rotten kids think this street is a raceway," and he went to the front window to check it out. He stared for a moment, then turned back to the table. "Is that your Corvette?"

"Yes, sir."

A low whistle broke the silence until her father returned to his seat. "Always wanted one of them."

The rest of the meal went smoothly. Her mother talked a lot about April as a child. Michael smiled and laughed at the humorous incidents she described. During dessert, Michael shared some highlights of the game Friday night and exchanged opinions with her father about the farm team, speculating who might get called up to Boston.

April rushed through the cleanup with her mother, then bowed out of staying any longer. "I'm afraid it's been a hectic week, Mom, and I was up late last night watching Michelle's kids."

"I understand. You need your rest. I hate to see you work so hard. Tell her she shouldn't work so hard, Michael."

"Believe me, I've tried. But she's got a mind of her own."

She kissed her mother. "Thanks, Mom. Dinner was great. Love you."

"Love you too. We'll see you next week. Please join her, Michael."

Uh-oh. Next week—the cruise. She shot a warning look at Michael.

"Uh, I won't be here next week, Mom. I'm . . . I'll be out of town . . . on business." *Rats, another lie . . . sort of.* She would be out of town, and it was more or less business, this deal between her and Michael.

"Oh, where are you going, honey?"

"Um, not sure yet. I won't know my travel details until later this week." There, that wasn't a lie.

"Okay. Be sure to let us know. Take care of yourself."

Michael stepped up with a small kiss to her mother's cheek. "Mrs. Vaillancourt, an absolute pleasure to meet you, and the next time we'll have to talk about my curtains. Mr. Vaillancourt, keep your Sox on."

When they got out to the car, April threw her head against the headrest. "Another lie!"

"Not exactly. You could have simply told her we were going on a weekend cruise and left out the details. You're a big girl—I doubt your mother would object."

No sense explaining to him how her mother would interpret that. If they went away together, that meant they were an item, a couple. She didn't want her mother to have any false hopes; God knows April had enough of her own. But once Michael got his promotion, their pretend marriage would be over, mission accomplished, and they'd go their separate ways. She didn't need her mother's questions as to why they weren't together anymore.

"Trust me, the lie was the better choice." She closed her eyes and waited for him to start the car. When he didn't, she turned to look at him.

"Why aren't you starting the car?"

He shrugged. "Wanna neck in your parents' driveway?"

She slugged his arm. "Why do you always joke when I'm frazzled?"

"Because I like to see you get fired up." He tweaked her cheek. "I did want to talk, though. I'm afraid we won't see much of each other this week. I have a full calendar of appointments, and two of them are lunch."

"That's okay, Michael. You don't owe me any explanation."

"No, but I'd like to have lunch with you on the days that I can. All right if I call your office when I'm free?"

She watched his dark eyes shimmer in the fading light. If only she could believe he really wanted to be with her, not just for how it looked to others.

"Yes, my schedule is lighter this week. Just let me know which days."

He rubbed a hand down her arm. "Thanks."

Her arm chilled the moment he released it. "And, Michael, thank you for being so great with my folks."

"That was easy. They're great people."

Another thing she'd have to hate him for later, when the charade was over.

Come Monday morning, Michael continued his routine of meeting April in the parking garage and walking her to the office building. He liked the bond he felt with her, acting as a couple.

But once he left her at the elevator, he forged ahead with nonstop meetings all day, and the same for the next. He managed a quick lunch with April on Wednesday and Thursday, and by the time Friday rolled around, he was ready for a relaxing cruise.

Michael emerged from his office at around eleven on Friday after two hours of conference calls. He knew there'd be a pile of messages waiting for him at Shelley's desk. After a quick trip to the men's room, he poured himself a fresh cup of coffee and braved his way to the receptionist.

"So, how is Mrs. Goode feeling these days?" Shelley's enthusiasm for juicy gossip never ceased. Once she'd gotten the notion of April's "secret" pregnancy into her head, she seized every opportunity to gush about it. He didn't have the heart to set her straight regarding her assumption, at least not right away.

"She's fine, Shelley." He took the stack of messages she handed over and began thumbing through them.

"Good, because she'll be jumping for joy when she hears the good news about your promotion."

Michael halted his message shuffling and stared at the grinning receptionist, who loved to be the first to relay any kind of news. "Promotion?"

Shelley wiggled excitedly in her seat, glanced down the hall to make sure no one heard, then leaned forward to whisper, "I heard Mr. Gellar dictating a memo. Apparently he's naming you his successor."

Michael straightened his shoulders, letting the information sink in. "Well, I'll be." He slowly turned toward his office. He needed to think, he needed a refuge, he needed—

"Michael! Here, you forgot your messages."

Without realizing it, he had dropped the pile back onto the reception desk. Odd, he wasn't prone to absentmindedness. But then, he'd never received such a mixed bag of news. Gellar was naming him to run the company, the one thing Michael had worked so hard for, yet he didn't feel the excitement he expected. He didn't feel as though he'd gained anything. In fact, it felt more like he'd lost something.

He reached his office, sat with a heavy thump in the leather executive chair, and swiveled it to look out at the city. Something was seriously off-kilter. He should be happy, bursting with pride, not glowering over what his promotion meant. And what was this overpowering sense of loss?

His gaze drifted to the manila envelope on the lower shelf of his bookcase. The album, the thing that had taken hold of his life and spun it around until he was exhilaratingly dizzy. Sadness gripped his heart because he knew what he was losing—the one thing he'd never had.

A wife.

April left work at noon on Friday to go home and pack. Since Monday, she and Michael had had little time to talk. Which was fine with her. The less she saw of him, the less she'd want him.

No, that wasn't true. She saw him in her dreams at night, in her ever-increasing daydreams, in the cuddly little teddy bear she'd rescued from the deflated balloon and propped on her desk. And she wanted him, still. More than ever.

But at least in his absence she didn't have to struggle to hide her feelings. And she would, until the end, when the deal was over and he got his promotion. Then she'd quietly fade into oblivion.

She set her suitcase near the door and checked the clock. Two. Michael said he'd pick her up at two, since the Gellars planned to set sail at four o'clock. No sooner had she thought it than a knock rattled her door.

The breathtaking sight of Michael Goode in khakis, a T-shirt, and boat shoes sans socks shook her reserve. She smiled at the man who looked at her with eyes as warm as her flushed cheeks. His own smile deepened the one-sided dimple she'd come to love.

"I'm all set." She nudged the big suitcase with her foot. "If you can grab that bag, I'll get this small one."

Michael stepped forward, but instead of picking up the bag, he slipped his hands around her waist and stilled the air with his presence.

"Don't you have a kiss for your husband?"

She tilted her head, determined not to play his little game outside of the playing field. "I'll save it for when it's really necessary."

His hands gripped her tighter, and his eyes burned brighter. "Oh, it's necessary, believe me." With that, he kissed her hungrily, and she responded helplessly.

Ever since she'd met him, Michael Goode had had that effect on her, willing her to do what she least expected and to enjoy every minute of it. She'd never once resisted his kisses, because she couldn't. They were magical. They left her wanting more.

Michael pulled back and licked his lips. "Mmm. That ought to hold me until we get to the car."

She swatted his arm. "Just pick up the bag, lover boy, before I change my mind."

He waggled his eyebrows as he released her. " 'Lover boy'?"

"Go!" she ordered, shooing him out the door while she shrugged on her jacket.

Michael cruised at a reasonable speed in the light traffic on the way to Newport, glad that the tourist season hadn't kicked in yet. The picture-perfect weather sent patchy puffs of clouds sailing across a sky so blue, it seemed to mirror the ocean.

With the sun beating down on his black Corvette, the interior quickly heated up, and April struggled out of her light jacket. Michael watched with interest, admiring the chic light blue knit top she wore over black Capri pants.

She finally settled back and asked, "Mind if I crack open the window?"

"Sure." He could use some cool air himself.

But he knew it wouldn't help. More than ever, April never left his mind lately. Friday night at the game now seemed far away, but he vividly remembered the heat of her lips as they kissed beneath the blanket.

"So how did all your meetings go?" she asked.

Glad to change the subject, he shifted his focus to work. "It's been a busy week despite the recent market fluctuations."

He talked about the long hours of negotiation with one client, the ups and downs of the market, even his rush to get out of the office that afternoon. April listened attentively, and Michael realized he'd never talked business with one of his dates before. Not that they wouldn't understand; he'd just never cared enough to open up.

It was so different with April. She made him forget about himself. He was completely relaxed, free to say anything, free to tell her exactly how he felt.

Well, not everything. At least not just yet.

"So how was your week?" he asked. "Did you get that new project tied up?"

"Yes, I finally nailed down the last details yesterday after fighting it all week. Tim said I spent a lot of time groaning."

"Why was this particular project so hard?"

"It wasn't so much the project. It was me. I had trouble focusing."

Michael slanted a hopeful look at her. "Oh? Something on your mind?"

She huffed at his insinuation. "Yeah, how I would get through this weekend."

He chuckled and slid his hand from the shift to pat her knee. "We'll think of something."

Chapter Fourteen

April had never been to the Newport Yacht Club. Why would she? Her blue-collar parents had eked out just enough to feed, clothe, and educate her, with little left over for luxuries. She'd had to work to help with her college tuition, but she didn't mind; it made her appreciate her success all the more.

After the Stan fiasco, moving into her own apartment had been the turning point for her career-oriented plan. She'd worked her way up and earned a reputation as a Web goddess. Tim had wasted no time snatching her from the big advertising firm where they'd both worked when he started Web Works. Even though he was the owner, they'd both built the business from the ground up and forged ahead.

But the price she'd paid was loneliness and having no one to share her life with. It had moved her to desperate measures, creating a fake wedding album and now pretending to be a wife. A sad ending for someone who'd had such high hopes for herself.

Michael lugged their bags to the dock and easily found the Gellars' yacht, one of the biggest on the waterfront. As soon as they stepped onto the gangway, Howard Gellar came out to greet them.

"Ahoy! Welcome aboard the *S.S. Reinvestment*." April laughed at the name. Leave it to Howard to make fun of himself. "My crew has been hard at work all day, and they say all systems are go for our first voyage this season. Come, I'll show you your cabin so you can put your things away and get back on deck for the cast off."

April took in the opulent surroundings of white, gold, and brass. Everything was as clean and shiny as though it had just been polished. Actually, it probably had. They walked around the teak deck and entered the deck salon lavishly furnished with cream-colored sofas, chairs, and cherrywood tables surrounded by walls of glass and mirrors.

They descended a winding staircase, then passed a state-of-the-art galley, where two staff members busily prepared what looked like a feast for an army. April inhaled the spicy aroma of something exotic, and her taste buds tingled, reminding her she hadn't eaten lunch.

Howard finally stopped at the end of the passageway and held open a large oak door with a brass knob and brass trim. "Your stateroom. Everything you need should be there. If not, just summon a crew member with this buzzer." He indicated the intercom box on the wall. "I'll leave you to get settled and see you topside in about ten minutes."

April eased slowly into the room, which looked like something out of a *Lifestyles of the Rich and Famous* episode. A private bathroom to the right, nearly as big as her living room, included double sinks, a walk-in shower, and a gold and white marble floor.

A thick hunter green carpet cushioned her feet in the bedroom and sitting area. Polished oak trimmed everything from the built-in cabinets to the minibar to the headboard. The floral print in the curtains, chair cushions, and pillow shams picked up the dark green of the rug.

But eventually her eyes settled on the green coverlet on the bed. No—more exactly, on the bed itself. The big, big bed.

The only bed.

Michael hoisted their bags on top of the coverlet and breathed a sigh of relief.

"Well, here we are, alone at last."

His casual remark rooted April to the spot. She'd known it would come to this but had somehow pushed it to the back of her mind to be dealt with later.

Later was here. Time to deal with it.

She skirted to the other side of the bed, opposite Michael, and lifted her small bag onto the mattress. His gaze followed her every movement.

"So, do you want to unpack?" he asked.

She shook her head.

"Want to shower?"

She shook her head more vigorously.

He slid down onto the bed, propping his hands behind his head as he leisurely stretched his long, lean body.

"Take a nap?"

Her eyes shot a warning at him.

"Okay, okay, I was just joking." He raised himself on his elbows. "But sooner or later, we'll have to sleep."

She tugged her personal bag over her shoulder and headed for the bathroom to busy herself unpacking toiletries. As she lined the exquisite marble countertop with her shampoo, toothpaste, brush, and makeup bag, she sensed Michael's shadow looming over her. Intimidated, she stuffed the bag with the remainder of her things under the counter, mindful that they'd be sharing this bathroom. Putting her personal items on display was more than she cared to reveal of herself right now.

"Forgive me." His mellow voice behind her soothed her fragile nerves. "I shouldn't have been so flippant."

"No, it's me. I'm just a bundle of nerves."

His strong hands covered her shoulders, and he turned her to face him. "I know. This isn't easy for you. Deceit is not in your vocabulary. But don't worry, this is all my doing, and I plan to make it up to you."

She leaned into his embrace, wishing she could tell him the one thing she wanted. Not tires, not jewelry, not expensive clothes, but something only he could give her.

Himself.

"Really, Michael, there's nothing I need."

He hugged her closely. With her cheek pressed against his chest, she faced the large wall-size mirror and caught her breath at the sight of their embrace while he gently rocked her.

"Ah, but there is. Remember when I told you I didn't want to just pretend, that I wanted to really get to know you? Well, I think I have, to the point where I think I know you better than you do. You'll see."

He stroked her hair, fiddling with a curl behind her ear. She watched his strong fingers twirl the delicate hairs with mesmerizing repetition.

Suddenly a ship's whistle blew, and an air horn split the tension in half. April tore herself from Michael, only to hear a low moan rumble in his throat.

"We'd better go topside," she warned reluctantly. "Sounds like we're about to set sail."

Even though it was May, the New England coastal region clung to patterns of cool ocean breezes and unpredictable temperature ranges. But Howard Gellar insisted they all stand on the flybridge during the launch, and April found herself shivering yet giddy with excitement.

The uppermost deck of the hundred-foot yacht afforded little protection against the chilly ocean air, but Michael Goode was all April needed. Standing behind her, he circled her with his warmth, his breath whispering past her ear making her shiver all the more.

She knew it was part of the show, part of the pretense of the happily married newlyweds. Yet being with him, being a part of him, made her feel complete. The hole in her life had been filled.

But she had to stop fooling herself. Michael Goode, the confirmed bachelor, thought of this as an adventure, another experience in his long line of women. He didn't commit to permanent relationships. He didn't need a woman to make him feel complete.

"Ah, this is the life," Howard sighed, hugging his wife too.

The sights of Newport's entire waterfront, complete with shops, historical landmarks, and glorious mansions, could be seen for miles. Air horns from other boats sounded as they pulled away while the occupants stood on deck to wave them off.

Connie Gellar enthusiastically waved to passing boats until they became mere specks behind them. Before long, they picked up speed and headed out to the open ocean, where only muted forms could be detected along the coast.

"We'll be heading south for warmer waters," Howard explained. "In the meantime, the sundeck below us is fully enclosed. Why don't we go down there?"

They made their way below to a salon area with great walls of glass that afforded a spectacular panoramic view along with heat. April brushed back her windblown hair, feeling the damp ocean mist on her cold fingertips.

"Oh, this is much better," Connie sighed. "Have a seat, and enjoy the view."

There were wicker chairs with plump cushions everywhere and a few stools in front of the corner oak bar, all complemented by a polished oak floor. But Michael wasted no time in ushering April to a two-seater bench along the wall. She sat uneasily at the edge until he settled next to her and drew her close to his side.

Connie Gellar smiled from across the round glass-top table between them. "Exactly how long have you two been married?"

"Six weeks." Michael's quick answer surprised April. She couldn't recall if they'd ever discussed their alleged wedding date with anyone.

"What a shame the wedding took place in Florida—I mean, for those of us up here. You must've been a beautiful bride and groom."

"April has family in Florida, so it just sort of happened when we were down there on vacation."

Connie sighed. "How romantic. I'd love to see the photos someday."

April stiffened under Michael's arm, but he held her closely and rubbed a reassuring palm against her shoulder.

"Absolutely."

April lost track of time as the yacht seemed to stand still in the endless surrounding of sea and sky. But the low hum of the engines affirmed they were still running, and the slowly changing scenery of the coastline on their right confirmed their forward movement.

She'd shed her jacket some time ago as the pleasant company and lively conversation negated any chill left in her bones.

Having Michael so close helped too. A couple of times he even brushed back her hair, letting his fingertips graze her cheek. She couldn't help but lean into them, closing her eyes to imagine he really meant it.

"You two make such a lovely couple," Connie crooned, adjusting her long skirt around her. The short, tapered style of her dark hair framed her delicate features like a harvested pearl. Still a handsome woman, she must've been a beauty in her day.

April smiled back. "We could say the same about you. You've obviously had a long and happy marriage."

Connie nodded. "Yes, overall it's been that. But there are always bumpy spots along the way. You just have to know how to handle them and go on until the road smooths out again."

"I'll keep that in mind," April asserted, slanting a look at Michael.

"Hey, no need to worry here, baby. I'm as smooth as they come."

Howard raised his glass. "That you are, my friend. But let me tell you one thing. . . ."

Connie rolled her eyes and gave a little shake of her head, warning April not to listen to the old fool's gibberish.

"This"—Howard pointed his finger toward April as he spoke to Michael—"is the most important investment you will ever make in your life. Treat it right, and your return will be tenfold."

Michael nodded and snuggled April closely. "I've already gotten back far more than I invested."

To her shock, he leaned down and kissed her fully on the lips while the Gellars looked on. She didn't know how much more playacting she could stand before she screamed her love for her accidental groom.

Somewhere through the fog in her brain, she heard a ship's bell, then the scraping of chairs on the salon floor.

"Well, dinner is ready," Howard announced. "I know I'm starving, but you two can stay here as long as you'd like." Then Howard and Connie left.

When Michael finally raised his head and gazed into her eyes, he laughed under his breath. "Phew. I'm not sure where that came from, but I think I'd like more." He kissed her again until she pushed him away with a decisive shove.

"I think we'd better be polite and join our hosts for dinner."
He groaned heavily. "But it's not food that I'm hungry for."

Seven courses later, April felt as stuffed as a Thanksgiving turkey and as pampered as a princess. She no sooner finished one dish than another was placed before her. And the dining room sparkled with gold lantern lights on cherrywood walls with a glass tube chandelier above the cherrywood dining table. Windows on both sides darkened as the sky changed from daylight to night, but small white lights twinkled along the railing outside, outlining the yacht against the dark sea.

She sat back, stretching her legs beneath the table to ease the discomfort of a full stomach. When she bumped Michael's leg with hers, he sent her a wink.

April couldn't ever remember being as happy as she was at that moment.

Clink, clink, clink. Howard Gellar stood as he tapped a spoon on the side of his wineglass. "Since we all seem to have had our fill, I'd like to say something before dessert is brought out."

April groaned at the thought of more food, and Michael licked his lips. Connie laughed at the two but cast her husband a questioning look.

"First of all, I'd like to say it is a pleasure to have such a friendly, loving couple on board with us. Something about the sea brings out the romantic in all of us, but especially in me." He paused to wave down the snickers from around the table. "I know, sometimes I appear to be this gruff old ogre who thinks, eats, and sleeps business. But there's another side of me, the side that appreciates beauty"—he tilted his glass to his wife—"tranquility"—a tilt to Michael—"and love"—the final tilt for April.

"Now that you've seen both sides, I have to tell you, I sometimes have trouble separating the two." An unexpected belly laugh bubbled out of Connie until the rest of them joined in. "Because of that quirk of my nature, I feel compelled to make an announcement that is work related." Again he paused to wave down the groan from Connie's side of the table. "This will be going out in a corporate memo next week, but right now I want just the four of us to celebrate the good news that, as of July 1, Michael Goode will be the new CEO of Gellar Investments."

Michael leaned on the deck rail to let the breeze slap his face into awareness. Ever since Howard's announcement, he'd felt numbed by a suffocating helplessness. He'd gone through the motions of accepting the congratulations, smiling, and thanking Howard for his faith in him.

But as he'd looked over at April, he knew something had changed. He saw the disappointment he'd feared would come when they achieved what they'd started out to do.

No. What *he* had started out to do. April had never wanted to be a part of it until he'd pushed her back to the wall and left her no option.

Which was why he'd planned to make everything right this weekend. He wanted to show her it wasn't about the promotion or about winning. It was about them and how he felt about her and how he knew she felt about him.

His intention had been to lay his cards on the table with her once and for all. Until Howard jumped the gun and set his plans afloat on the open sea.

The air stirred behind him, then beside him, as April took a spot at the rail. "Where's Howard?"

"He finished his cigar and went below. Said it was too cold for his old bones."

April crossed her arms tightly. "It's cold for bones of any age. You must be freezing."

He swung his arm around her to lend her some heat. "Nah, I've hardly noticed. Been too busy thinking."

"You do have a lot to think about. You'll soon be running that company, Michael. That's a big responsibility."

"Oh, it's nothing I can't handle."

"Then why aren't you down there celebrating? Why aren't you and Howard huddled in a strategy session? This is what you wanted, isn't it?"

He turned sideways and pivoted her to face him. Even in the dark of night, her blue eyes shone brighter than any sky he'd ever seen. Her blond curls waved in the wind. She was a vision he hadn't been able to get out of his mind since the day he saw that wedding album.

"It's what I thought I wanted. But now that it's here . . . I don't know. It seems more like a consolation prize."

"That's because you're a hunter, Michael. For people like you, the thrill is in the chase, in doing what it takes to make the kill. When you've reached your goal, when it's within reach, the thrill is gone, and you need to move on to the next hunt."

He studied the sadness that had crept into her eyes. He didn't like it; he wanted to make her happy. Today and always.

"Maybe the promotion wasn't what I really wanted."

She shook her curls back. "It was. You just got sidetracked into thinking it was a game, like the game we've been playing. Unlike your games in business, which will continue on as many small hunts, our game is over. We've accomplished our objective, and now we can go our separate ways."

He grabbed her shoulders and pulled her tightly to him. "No! I don't want it to end."

She swallowed hard, and her voice cracked. "Michael, let go."

Chastising himself for his rough reaction, he immediately released her.

She shook her head. "I meant let go of the game. We had a deal. I'd play your wife until you got the promotion. Now I have a life and a career to get back to."

He raised his hands to frame her face. "But that life doesn't include a husband."

"No, it doesn't. And I'll never get one if I keep wasting my time on foolishness such as this."

She stepped back and waited for him to respond, but he couldn't seem to recover from that unexpected slap in the face. What he'd meant to say was that her other life didn't include a husband, while this one did. And this husband wanted to make her happy with every last ounce of his strength.

She finally turned away, her shoulders noticeably slumped. "It's been a long day. I'm going to bed."

Michael reluctantly let her leave, knowing that any argument he confronted her with now would only seem empty and desperate. He needed to regroup his thoughts, come up with a better plan. If this were business, he'd have a solution in a snap, but when it came to love, what did he know?

With his elbows on the rail, he roughly raked his hands through his hair, pulling until the roots hurt. Nothing in his wide experience had prepared him to salvage a marriage and a new job when he'd screwed up both before they even began. For once he was on unfamiliar ground.

April got into the shower as quickly as she could to wash away tears she hadn't wanted to shed. That pigheaded man, the investment genius, didn't know when to fold or when to lay down a winning hand. Even with the promotion in his back pocket, he still wasn't happy. And nothing she said made any difference.

The tears were for herself, though, angry tears because she'd gotten exactly what she didn't want—a broken heart. Would she ever learn? Her friends would never believe it. The desperate bride who'd created a groom, fallen in love with him, then lost him to a mistress—his job.

April's fool.

After her shower, she slipped into a nightgown, then wrapped herself in one of the thick white terry robes that hung in the closet. A gold embroidered *G* insignia boasted the Gellar yacht. For company, she grabbed a book from her bag and climbed into bed.

Minutes went by without her reading more than a sentence. None of the words made sense. Nothing in her head made sense. She wished she could get up and leave the yacht, the Gellars, and Michael Goode far behind. But taxi service in the middle of the Atlantic Ocean was impossible and explaining the problem to the Gellars even harder.

A noise at the door grabbed her attention. Michael entered, peering around the door as though danger stood behind it. Since she'd turned off all the lights except the bedside lamp, she could only make out his silhouette, but he appeared to be tiptoeing.

"It's okay, I'm awake," she called from across the gigantic luxury cabin.

He looked up and approached the bed with slow, calculated steps. "I'm sorry if I said anything to offend you up there. Things happened so fast, I was a little confused as to which direction I'm headed in."

"Up."

He tilted his head and frowned at her. "Up what?"

"You're headed up. Up the corporate ladder, up to an even more successful career."

With a slight acknowledging nod, he sank down onto a corner of the mattress at the foot of the bed. "I always knew that. It was a given. It's my personal life I'm unsure of."

April closed her book and waited. She'd never seen him so morose, so tentative. Even his shoulders slumped with less assurance.

"I've always thought of myself as a bachelor, never the marrying kind. But these last few weeks with you have been eye-opening. I never realized how much I needed to share personal feelings. Having someone to talk to was so freeing. And you cared, April. You listened and cared."

She drew up her knees beneath the covers and leaned on them. "Of course I cared. I care about you."

He leaned forward, shortening the gap on the empty part of the bed. "Then why can't we make this work? Why can't we give it a chance?"

She sucked in her breath at what he asked, but the feeling was missing. She knew what he meant, but the words were all wrong.

"Because this is not what a marriage is built on. Fabrication, untruths, misrepresentation." She waved her left hand in front of her face. "Meaningless rings." Michael winced. "When I enter into a marriage, I want it to be for love. I want to be hit over the head with it. I want to be swept off my feet. I want passion and tenderness and a man who adores me for who I am, not for someone he's made me."

He seemed to shrink back. "And you don't think I can be that man or do any of those things?"

She sighed. The night had taken its toll on her weary soul. She knew he could be all that and more, but he had to believe it and want it more than anything. He had to understand that more than just empty words or material things brought two people together. He needed to discover what his heart wanted.

"All I know is, we had a bad start, and it brought us to the uncertain crossroads we're at now. Talking it to death will get us nowhere tonight. I'm tired, and if you don't mind, I'd like to sleep."

He nodded in agreement and left to dig some things out of his bag. April slid deeper under the covers and listened as he went into the bathroom and prepared for bed. When he came out in gray sweatpants, he took a pillow from the bed and checked the closet for a blanket. She turned to see him preparing a makeshift bed on the sofa.

Guilt-ridden, she called out softly, "Michael, this bed is plenty big for both of us. You don't have to sleep on the sofa." His face briefly lit up, and a smile widened his lips until she added, "As long as you stay on your side of the bed and *above* the covers."

Chapter Fifteen

April awoke to the warm sensation of a strong arm across her stomach, a chin nestled on her shoulder, and steady breathing against her cheek. She sighed inwardly, snuggling closer.

When reality shook her fully awake, her eyes flew open, and she turned her head with a start. There she was on the opposite side of the bed from where she'd started the night before, in the arms of a smiling Michael Goode.

Clutching the covers, she pushed away. "What are you doing?" she asked sharply.

His dimple deepened. "Watching you sleep."

"Why were you . . . hugging me? You were supposed to stay on your side of the bed."

"I did. *You* came over to my side." She bit her lip, examining her place in the bed. He was right. "And as you can see, I'm still above the covers, and you're under them."

"Oh. I guess I do move around a lot in bed." She smiled shyly as she realized how comical she must look in her thick terry robe hidden under the covers.

"Yes, and you also groan a lot, like Tim said."

She rubbed her eyes. "What time is it?"

He checked the bedside clock. "Seven." She groaned. "See? That's what you do in your sleep." She rolled back to her side of the bed and tugged the covers up around her neck. "I was thinking of checking out the exercise room. Care to join me?"

"No way. You go, have a good time."

He whistled his way to the bathroom and continued the merry

tune in there. Without a doubt, he was a morning person, unlike her. When he came out, he wore shorts, a T-shirt, and a smile from ear to ear.

"You're in an awfully good mood this morning. Where's the morose guy who slinked in here last night?"

He flashed his dimpled side to her. "He was up a good part of the night, thinking. Today is a new day, and he has a new plan."

April groaned again and pulled the covers over her head. "Please tell me it doesn't include me."

When he didn't answer, she peeked over the blankets and was startled to see him standing just above her at the side of the bed. He ducked down quickly and gave her a peck on the forehead.

"We'll see."

He flung a towel over his shoulder and sauntered out of the cabin, whistling again.

Invigorated from his workout in the Gellars' state-of-the-art exercise room, Michael jogged back to the cabin with his fresh plan in place and the renewed vigor to set it into motion. His new goal challenged him in a completely different way than any other. But when it came to April, she was worth it.

She wanted love; she wanted to be swept off her feet. He could do all of that. He could be everything she wanted him to be.

And he would.

He entered the cabin and smiled at the seemingly tiny lump in the middle of such a huge bed. She stirred slightly.

"It's just me," he called. "I'll be in the shower."

The only response was a low moan. She really loved her sleep.

By the time he came out of the shower, she'd opened her eyes enough for him to see the blueness blinking at him. She raised her head and sent him an inquisitive look. "Shorts? Won't you be cold?"

"No, it's gorgeous out there. I guess we traveled far enough south during the night, the temperature is much warmer." He pressed one of the buttons on the intercom.

"What are you doing?" she asked, sitting up higher.

"I met Howard in the passageway. He said to press that button, and one of the crew would bring a coffee tray. Full breakfast is ready in the dining room whenever we want."

"Oh, that sounds yummy." Her eyes seemed to open wider, and a stiff yawn stretched her sleep-puffy lips. She shook her head back, letting her hair fall over her shoulders.

He stood there motionless, admiring how someone so tousled could look so beautiful. That's why he'd been staring at her early this morning, imagining what it would be like to wake up that way every day. He wanted to reach out and run his fingers through her untamed curls and taste those inviting lips.

But that would have to wait. There'd be plenty of mornings for him to do that, he hoped. All good things in their own time.

"Okay." She rolled and rolled until she reached the edge of the bed. "I'll just take a quick shower. You can go for breakfast if you'd like."

"No, I'll wait for you."

A light knock at the door startled her. She gripped her robe closer around her neck. Michael opened the door and allowed the man with the coffee cart to station it in the alcove by the windows.

April's eyes widened in awe after the man left. "That's a coffee tray?" She padded over to inspect the assortment of muffins, danish, fruit, teas, and coffees. "We don't even need to leave the room!"

Michael took her arm and prompted her toward the bathroom. "*Yes,* we do. Now go shower, and we'll go topside for the full breakfast."

She pouted as she dug in her suitcase for her black stretch pants and a white jersey top. "At least pour me a coffee. Please."

He smiled brightly. "Anything for you."

With her clothes draped over her arm, she took a steaming cup from him and retreated to the bathroom. Michael sat at the table in the alcove and savored a black coffee.

His thoughts strayed to the future and the life he wanted to share with April. They'd started out on shaky ground and a lot of false pretenses. He was about to change all that. She needed more than just shallow words and empty promises, a lot more.

He could give her that.

Yes, he could.

April smiled into the shower spray. In her head she replayed her waking moments that morning, Michael's dimpled grin and the warmth of his breath against her cheek.

But his eyes had smiled down at her, caressed her with something she hadn't noticed before. Love? Did he feel love for her? Did he know what love was? Did she know how love felt in return?

And what was that business about a new plan? How would it affect her? Her brain had been too muddled with sleep to bother thinking about it till now.

In business, Michael always had to be ready with an alternate plan should something go wrong. In this case, what could be the alternative to a job promotion based on a phony marriage? Of one thing she was certain: she wouldn't agree to any extension of the marriage sham, no matter what he offered.

She shook her head to clear the confusion. After breakfast, she'd pin him down for exact details of his new plan.

Refreshed and wide awake, she left the bathroom eager to start their last day together but stopped when she caught sight of Michael sitting in the sunlight, staring out at the ocean with a satisfied smile on his face. A thick lump formed in her throat. If only she could wake up to that every day, she'd die a happy woman.

He stood when he heard her approach, and she had to force the lump down in order to speak. Those powerful legs she remembered from their run on the bike path now took quick strides toward her. With his green polo shirt and tan shorts, he looked as casual as a *GQ* model, only twice as handsome.

"Okay, I'm ready."

He met her at the foot of the bed. "We don't have to go right away. We can sit and enjoy some time to ourselves first."

She glanced over at the inviting cart. "That muffin over there does look pretty appetizing."

He laughed, and they went to take seats on opposite sides of the small marble table. He poured coffee. She buttered her muffin. No words were spoken, just an exchange of appreciative glances and knowing looks. Michael sipped his coffee slowly and looked completely at ease with the company and the quiet.

"So what's this big plan you have?"

A slight twitch in his cheek seemed to signal the end of his daydream as his face tightened and he blinked several times before answering.

"You'll have to be patient. You'll know when the time comes."

"Hmm, the last time you sprang one of your plans on me, I almost needed a paramedic." Remembering back to that night in his office when he presented the wedding album still sent chills down her spine.

"Ah, but think of *my* shock when I received that wedding album. It was like the kiss of death to this confirmed bachelor."

A rope tightened around her heart. He admittedly still clung to the label. The bachelor. Maybe that was part of his new plan— he'd figured out a way to save face with Howard and dissolve this senseless fake marriage.

"Yes, but you didn't waste any time taking advantage of the situation and using it to your benefit." Her accusation bit a little harder than she had intended.

Unaffected, Michael tipped his head. "Guilty on all counts. But that's my nature—make the best of what comes your way. Throw stones at me, and I'll use them to build a wall."

April laughed. "Those hands have never done a day's hard labor in your life."

"I beg your pardon. I wasn't born with a silver spoon in my mouth, you know. I had my share of menial jobs in high school and college."

"Really? I'd like to hear that story."

He put down his coffee. "Some other time. Let's go up to breakfast now and see if the Gellars are about."

April took a last gulp of her coffee and got up to join Michael at the cabin door. With his back to the door, he looked her in the eye, and she swore he stared right through her soul.

"April, one thing before we go."

"Yes?"

As though a demon had suddenly possessed his body, he reached for her, pulled her tightly to his chest, and proceeded to kiss her with a fervor she'd never experienced from any man. His arms wrapped tighter around her back. His smoothly shaven face glided along her cheek, no raspy whiskers to scrape or irritate. He smelled deliciously fresh from the shower. Only his low moans could be heard above the pounding of her heart.

When his kiss finally slowed, he put his hands to her face and pulled away. He licked his lips and exhaled heavily.

"Remember that," he whispered.

As though he knew the immobilizing effect his kiss had had on her, he took her hand and led her—almost dragged her—out the door and up to the dining room.

Was that a good-bye kiss? *Remember that?* What did that mean? Was he daring her to find someone else who even came close to kissing like him? Was that his way of saying thanks for the memories?

They stepped into the dining room to find the Gellars just taking their seats.

"Good morning! Well, it looks like we old folks beat you young ones to the table. Everything okay? Everyone sleep well?"

Michael held out the big cushioned chair for April opposite Connie Gellar. "Yes, couldn't have been more comfortable," he replied with a wink to April.

She blushed, remembering her contentment waking up curled in Michael's arms and snuggled to his body. Then she blushed even more when she realized what the Gellars must have been thinking about her blush!

In an attempt to cover up, she blurted, "Two people could get lost in that bed." Six eyes turned to her, followed by three smiles. She wanted to bite off her tongue.

Michael reached over, covered her hand with his, and murmured for the benefit of the Gellars, "Yes, but we managed to find each other."

Connie gave her a sweet smile, and Howard looked as pleased as punch. Michael's sparkling eyes held her gaze until, flustered beyond repair, April dipped her head and dug into the fruit plate set before her.

Once again, the staff silently served dish after dish as the four of them talked about the beauty of the ocean on a sunny day and how completely relaxing a day at sea could be. April found herself talking about her childhood, her college years, and her big step of moving out on her own.

"That was awfully courageous," Connie gasped. "I went right from my father's house to my husband's, and that was scary enough!" They all laughed.

"Speaking of moving," Howard added, "will you two be buying a house or staying in that condo?"

April cast a wide-eyed look of panic to Michael, who, as usual, didn't have a single feather ruffled. As calm as could be, he stood and cleared his throat to call the table to attention.

"I think this would be a good time to make a few announcements and get a few facts straight. First of all, we are ever so grateful for your generous invitation to join you this weekend on your magnificent floating palace. It's a trip I know I won't soon forget." Howard and Connie nodded graciously like doting parents. "Connie, you are grace and elegance personified, and no matter how old you turned a few weeks ago, I won't believe it."

Laughter roared from Howard, and Connie tittered bashfully. April clenched her napkin as she studied Michael, wondering why the grand gesture, sensing an impending cloud of doom.

"Howard, you know how I admire you. You've been not only a mentor, but almost a father. Gellar Investments has been a home to me, and I've never regretted a moment of my time there."

He paused, and April thought she heard something like the low roll of thunder before it crashes around your head.

"Until now."

Connie gasped.

Howard stiffened in his seat.

April tried to slink under the table.

"Respectfully, I'm afraid I must decline the promotion to CEO of Gellar Investments."

"What?"

"What?"

"What?"

The question was unanimous.

"I've done something I'm not altogether proud of, but I want to set the record straight now before anyone gets hurt."

He left his place at the table and turned to April, gently lifting her left hand as though it might break. His eyes captured hers for a moment, sending a sad message she didn't quite understand. He then grasped the wedding ring and carefully slid it off the end of her finger.

Holding the ring up between thumb and forefinger, he turned to Howard. "This is not real, or, rather, what it represents is not real. April and I are not really married. There's a very long story as to how it all came about, but it all boils down to the fact that it was my idea to pretend we were married in order to put me in good favor with you. I wanted that promotion more than anything in the world, and I was determined to show you what a stable, reliable employee I was."

He ceremoniously set the ring down on the table.

April clenched her hands in front of her mouth, biting on her finger to waken herself from this bad dream. Howard ran a tired hand down his face, the lines around his mouth deepening with disappointment.

"I regret any embarrassment this may cause you, and if you request it, I will have my resignation on your desk Monday morning."

"Now, just hold on a minute." Howard's voice rose almost to a bellow. "I'm not sure I understand the logic for refusing this promotion or even resigning altogether."

"I deceived you, Howard, and I let you down."

"How did you let me down?"

"By making a mockery of your principles."

Howard scratched the side of his head. "And how exactly did you mock my principles?"

"Everyone knows how you feel about your key people being married, having a stable family life."

"Really? Just like everyone knows about April's pregnancy?"

"What? I'm not pregnant!" April declared vehemently.

"I *know* that, my dear. I'm just making a point. People talk around an office, and most of the time it's nonsense. Michael, do you really think I'm so shallow as to promote someone because he's married, or not promote him because he's a bachelor? Give me some credit here. I didn't make it to where I am today by such narrow-minded thinking."

"Well, thank you, sir. It's good to know you have that confidence in me. But, still, after what has happened, I wouldn't fault you for turning over the reins to Kenny. He'd be a worthwhile choice."

"He'd be an abomination!" Howard slapped his hand onto the table, making the ring bounce. Michael snapped it up before it fell. "Kenny Gellar may be my nephew, but he's only half the man you are, Michael. I'd stay in that position until I died rather than turn it over to that lazy bundle of bones."

April tensed in her seat as she witnessed this new side of Howard Gellar unfolding. But Connie stifled a chuckle, and April realized that letting off steam was part of Howard's nature.

"This is ridiculous," Howard grumbled. "I can't believe we're even discussing Kenny over you. And furthermore, this business about you two not being married . . . well, if you're not, then you should be. I have eyes. I know what love is. Now, put that ring back onto her finger, and let's forget all about this."

"I'm afraid I can't do that, sir."

April felt her heart sink somewhere down near her toes. He was going to drop her right here, right now, in front of their hosts. Game over. No score.

Howard glared menacingly at Michael and started to point a finger.

"Before you say anything, Howard, I'd like to explain one more thing. I said before that I wanted that promotion more than anything in the world, and that was true. Until I found April."

She felt as though someone had just sent a jolt of electricity through her chair. What was he doing? Was this the new plan?

He turned back to her. "April, darling, these last few weeks with you have been the happiest of my life. Even though we weren't truly married, I believed it—I *felt* it. When Howard offered me that promotion last night, all I could think about was losing you, because if the pretense was over, then you'd be gone, and I couldn't live with that. I want you in my life, every day, for the rest of my life. This ring was put on your finger for the wrong reason."

He set the wedding band down again, then reached into his pocket. Gingerly he held up another gold band with a proud diamond mounted on top.

"But this ring is for the right reason. It's because I love you. It's because I want us to be together always. It's because I want you to accept me as your husband, for real."

Michael knelt down before April and slid the ring onto her naked ring finger. "April Vaillancourt, will you be my wife?"

Connie Gellar gasped. Howard squirmed in his chair. April opened her mouth, closed it, opened it again. She tried to speak, but no words came out. He'd done it; he'd actually done what he said he could do.

He'd swept her off her feet.

She shook her head from side to side, staring at the ring, waiting for something to happen, until she realized everyone was waiting for *her* to speak.

"Michael, this is unreal. We're in the middle of the ocean. Where did you get a diamond ring?"

Michael smiled, his loving smile, his brown-eyed killer smile. "My April. Always looking for the logical explanation. Sweetheart, I'd already planned to propose to you during this trip, just not so abruptly. But Howard's surprise announcement last night sort of threw everything out of sequence. I didn't want to lie anymore. I wanted us to be married before the promotion was settled. And I was afraid if I took the promotion and proposed afterward, you'd think I was trying to save face. But the truth is, you mean more to me than any promotion, and if I can have only one or the other, I choose you."

A lifetime of dreaming passed before her eyes. Michael Goode was her prince, her knight in shining armor, her every fantasy come true. Tears stung her eyes as she captured the feeling of being loved completely. She closed her eyes and let it wash over her like the sun's rays coming out from behind a cloud.

Michael shook her ring finger slightly; he still held it between his. "April, you haven't answered me. Are you thinking about it?"

She opened her eyes and gazed down at the obscenely large diamond on her finger. "You were quite sure of yourself, weren't you?"

His dimple seemed to wink at her. "You know me, always sure of myself. But this time I need you to say it, love. Will you marry me? Will you be my wife for all eternity?"

April nodded and whispered a faint "Yes." Connie released a strangled cry of relief, and Howard applauded as Michael took April in his arms and kissed her with the love of a husband. A real husband.

She didn't know how long they kissed, but eventually the sound of Howard loudly clearing his throat broke through the haze of their love.

"I'm glad we got that settled," he said with great relief. "Now, about that resignation . . ."

Michael rose from his knee but continued to hold April's hand. "As I said, you can have it first thing Monday morning."

"Not a chance. If we have to, we'll stay on this yacht until you come to your senses. Do you really want to make your bride wait that long for her wedding day?"

Michael pulled April up into his arms and gazed longingly into her eyes. "*I'm* the one who can't wait. I'd be a fool to put it off any longer." He kissed her softly and whispered, "April's fool."

Epilogue

April paced from the living room to the kitchen and back, not a very big area in her small apartment, and not altogether comfortable in high heels.

Where was Michael? The last thing she wanted was to be late for their engagement party, which the Gellars had insisted on lavishing upon them.

Finally, a knock.

"Where've you been? I was worried sick. We're going to be late." She'd blurted her concerns before the door was even half-open.

Michael stepped forward and took his bride-to-be in his arms and kissed her with the fervent desire she'd come to relish since their engagement on the cruise.

"Hello to you too," he teased. Then, with his usual self-assured smile he added calmly, "I just needed to run a quick errand. Don't worry, the party will wait for us. We're the guests of honor."

"Oh, right," she said with a sheepish shrug. She lingered in his arms a moment longer, content to remain that way for the rest of her life.

They locked up her apartment and went down to the street. April looked up and down the curb, puzzled that his car was nowhere to be seen.

"Where's your Vette?"

"I let your father drive it to the party. He's always wanted a Corvette, remember?"

She laughed. "Oh, he sure has. That must've made his day. So, I guess we take my car, then?" She started for the back lot.

"Yes, we do," Michael said, jingling a set of keys.

185

April turned back to see Michael at the curb, a set of keys dangling from his fingers, and his other hand pointing to a new red SUV.

"I know it's bigger than you're used to, but you'll need it for the kids and toys and dogs—"

"You bought me a car?"

"Hey, we had a deal. New tires, remember?"